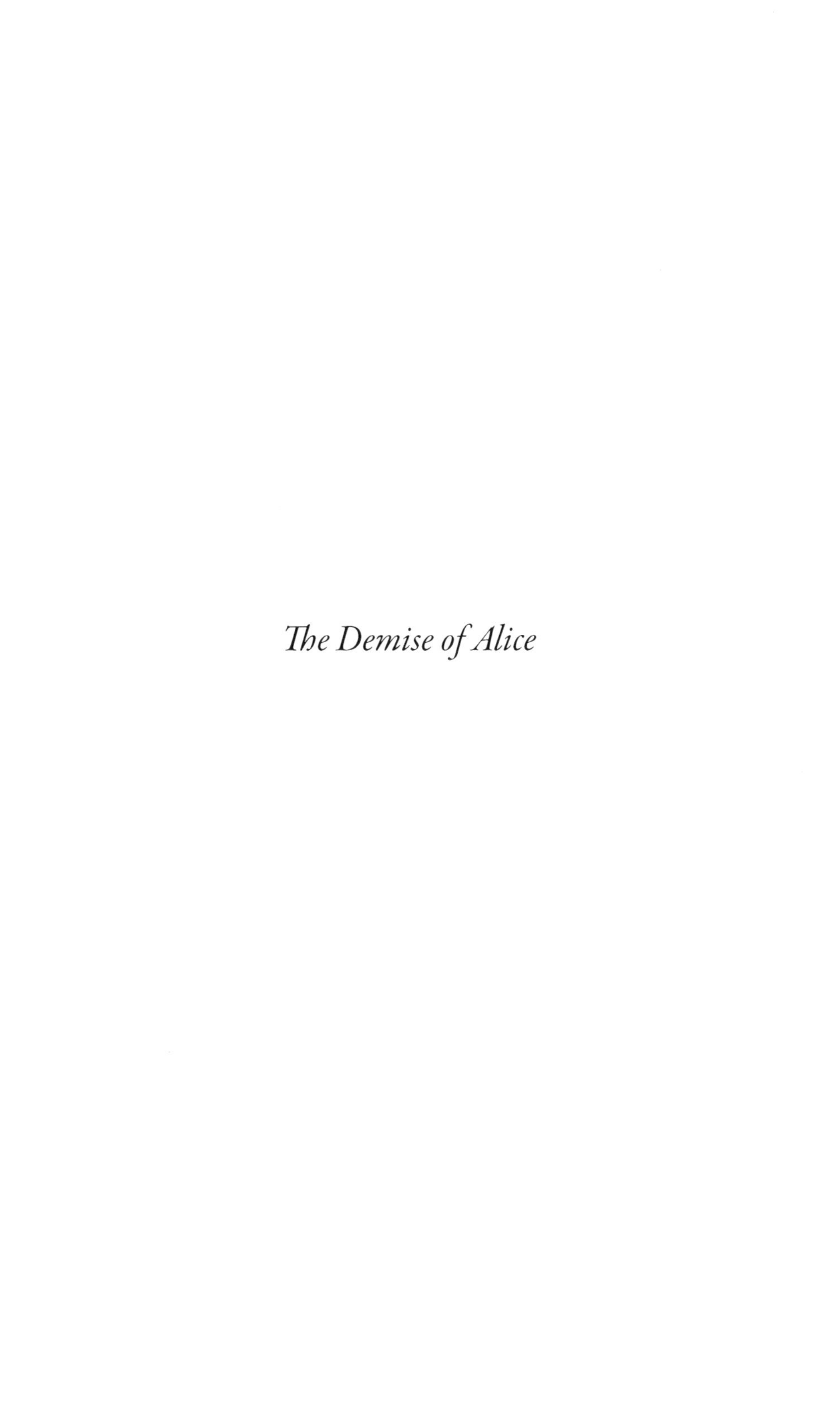

The Demise of Alice

The Demise of Alice

a

Grace Hannah Perez

novel

by

Evelyn Grace Vex

Dissolve Publishing
San Francisco, CA & Brooklyn, NY

Cover photograph by Judd Dunning.
Tree of Life by Grace Hannah Perez, 2023.
Photograph of Grace Hannah Perez and Ava Perez by Judd Dunning, c. 2016–2017.
Photograph of Grace Hannah Perez, Abney Park Cemetery, London, 2018.

First edition: Self-published by the author in 2020.
Second edition: First published as a Dissolve Book in 2024.

Title: The Demise of Alice / Evelyn Grace Vex, Grace Hannah Perez.
Names: Vex, Evelyn Grace, author (pseudonym) | Perez, Grace Hannah, 2000–2023, author.
Published: San Francisco & Brooklyn : Dissolve Publishing, 2024.
Library of Congress Control Number: 2024930369
LC record available at https://lccn.loc.gov/2024930369
ISBN: 978-1-963280-99-9

Cover and interior design by Dissolve Publishing.
Typesetting by Christopher Squier.
Copy edits by Christopher Squier & Jackie Valle.

10 9 8 7 6 5 4 3 2 1

Dissolve Publishing
San Francisco, CA & Brooklyn, NY
http://dissolvesf.org

Dissolve is an art collective and curatorial project where art-making and looking are personal, performative, entangled, and unexpected. We attend to the ruptures and fissures in culture, where art flourishes. Dissolve is a project by Kathryn Barulich, Christopher Squier, and Jackie Valle.

Editors' Note

The Demise of Alice commences with Alice's first victim, Luther. In fact, the novel's first act of violence is lodged within its first ten pages, while the bulk of the narrative is devoted to deciphering the meaning of this event. For Alice, Luther is a stranger, a potential lover, and in a murderous blackout fueled by bootlegged alcohol, the appearance of a butcher knife, and fatalism—a potential mark. Alice is the daughter of a known mobster, the infamous man around town, Benjamin W., whose own occult practices seem to drive many of Alice's most destructive impulses. Following Luther's murder, a blending of victim and perpetrator draws the novel into territory reminiscent of the guilt-ridden narrators of *Crime and Punishment* or *The Tell-Tale Heart*, yet with a specificity unique to its author: here, our protagonist is a painfully thin fifteen-year-old girl, at once a tenacious detective and a potent femme fatale. When an uncannily familiar face whose eyes "resemble dark holes shot through his head" returns to Alice as if "out of thin air," she finds herself bound to an obligation to investigate the murder of her own doing, falsifying the record as she goes. In her encounters with action and avoidance, agony, guilt, and shame, Alice leads us in an exploration of the often painful discord of adolescence as she examines the world through eyes that are weary and wise, desperate, thoughtful, and hopeful for other futures.

Alice committed a murder, but she is no murderer—a label that haunts her throughout the novel and which she tries frequently to buck. However, she is an adept observer, watching from her balcony late into the evenings and stationed at the last seat, her favorite, at the bar of her father's speakeasy Vex. She investigates a crime of her own devices in order to expose and explain the strange and complex brutality that exists in society's shadow. And for an observer of humanity's paradoxical cruelties, what better setting than her sultry, corrupt, illicit, and downright rotten hometown of 1920s New Orleans?

It is this capacity for observation and fabulation which she shares with Evelyn Grace Vex, the nom de plume Grace Hannah Perez assigns to her book's author. Contemplating passersby in the street, she writes, "This could be completely untrue of course, yet I often love to give stories to strangers, if only to make the world seem a little less awful." Here, perhaps, is where Perez's impulse to write meets her character's desire to escape the violence of her life: both aim to produce a surplus of meaning for the world, a glistening cobweb of fantasies and speculations that make the world less dark, and this capacity for observation extends beyond the underside of human impulse to the equally confounding order of its ideals, chief among those, love. As Alice falls deeper into the trap of her own making, she also finds herself bound by love to the person she knows is most justified in rejecting her affection, one who will likely lead her to doom.

Early on in the novel, Alice remarks that the concept of time has always baffled her. She wonders how time was invented, placing her father's pocket watch in the freezer "so I could stop time." Needless to say, her experimental mindset displeased her father; later in the novel, we come to understand Benjamin's own reasons for wanting to sidestep the past and postpone its bitter aftertaste. In its scrutiny of time and death, the novel is also in conversation with Mary Shelley's *Frankenstein*, offering a rebuke of man's unethical compulsion to play at God. It is an irony of the novel that perhaps its most brutal character, a megalomaniacal scientist named Clyde, offers the shrewdest take on the irretrievability of time: "The world is changing with each passing moment," he counsels Alice, "and oftentimes the most unexpected gifts can be the ones right in front of us."

We extend our gratitude to the family of Grace Hannah Perez, especially to her parents Angela Cordova Dunning and Judd Dunning and her sister Ava Perez, for their generosity, support, and trust with Perez's manuscript. To Natasha Lake, we share our deep thanks for loaning your copy of Perez's original, self-published edition. It has been an honor to memorialize Perez and steward this indelible project.

When I die
I want whoever reads this to
Know my life was very fulfilling.
And I love so many people.
Even if I don't know you that well,
There's a good chance
I love you....

—*Grace Hannah Perez, 2020*

Grace H. Perez

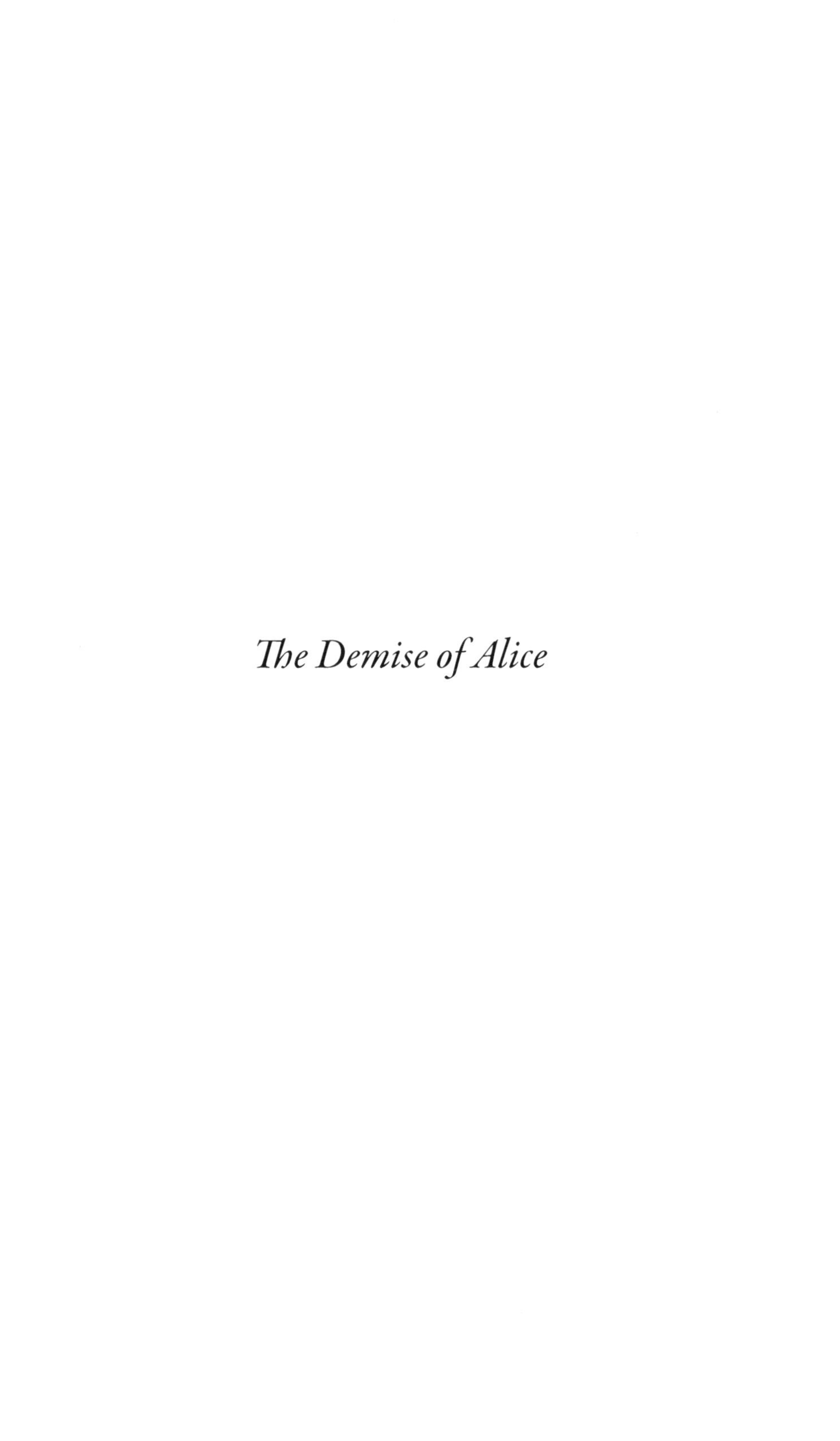

The Demise of Alice

For Ava
The Only One

I

I WATCH him watching me. He's youthful, lustful, and my personal favorite, timid. It is 1927, the age of innocence, and virtue has long passed, leaving only the rotten and filthy to rule the times. Speakeasies populate the city of New Orleans and, with no one bothering to abide by the rules any longer, the city has fallen victim to all that is nefarious. It can be said that my father is one of the many men to have furthered the corruption around the city, seeing as Vex, his speakeasy, is the most well-known in the town. Vex is filled to the corners tonight with the usual faux-glamor flappers, cheap whores, and gentlemen who aren't gentle.

This is where I was raised, among the wrongdoers of society, the eccentric, and the talented. That is all that I can recall of anything in life this far and, to those surrounding me, it seems to be their place of choice. They delight in the smoke which envelops us all in the room, serving its very purpose. It's a ruse, a mere illusion, an enticing mood that keeps the occupants of the club coming back for more and thinking it is of their own accord. They dance their bodies senseless to the sounds of trombones and saxophones or lounge on the sweat and bloodstained Victorian love seats while finding pleasure in any warm-blooded human. Just as I'm about to, with him.

Yes, the tall, lanky boy with his face sunken in and those lost eyes. So lost, just looking for a lithe, young thing such as me to guide him to shore. I drum my fingers impatiently on the wooden table as I down my glass of gin in one sip and begin to stand up. The burning liquid makes its way down my throat; I feel nothing. I've only had two drinks tonight and it takes twice that amount to acquire the effect I desire.

I lock eyes with him as I walk toward him, my heart beating in coordination with each step. He is even more captivating than I had perceived. He is shy though; it is evident in his eyes. I love the shy ones. They remind me of my youth, hiding behind my father's broad-built shoulders and sinister tone. As if a gangster for a father was some sort of hero—hardly. Though I will tell you, it's a hell of a lot easier to scare people. But I didn't want to scare this one. Not yet.

"Hi," I say, as my lips part in amusement. He studies me, his eyes searching me from my black drop-waist to my tan stockings reaching high enough to be indecent. The only thing I had not put on display was my garter belt. He'd find that out later though.

"I'm Luther," he says.

"Alice," I respond.

"How's your night tonight?"

I let out a sigh as I looked over my shoulder at a woman trying to dance who was obviously too intoxicated to keep her footing.

"Uneventful," I respond. I reach over, snatching the cigarette from his lips and inhaling the fumes. "Thank God," I say. "I've been looking for one of these all night."

"Well, I'm glad I could be of use."

Now it's my turn to examine him. He's physically alluring, yet holds a calmness that I cannot stand. I begin searching around the room again, trying to decipher the crowd to see if there are any other eligible suitors, when he interrupts my thoughts.

"Can I get you a drink?"

I give him a wicked smile. He has captured my attention once again. There's nothing I love more than alcohol, the way I get lightheaded and all the little things I despise about the world seem to evaporate into thin air. We walk over to the bar and Luther sets out some cash in front of the bartender, Jack.

Jack is in his mid-thirties with dark eyes and messy brown hair. He was much more handsome when he was younger, I assume, yet his charm has not faltered an inch. Jack has grown as I have, the years only bringing more discontent with the comings and goings of people who sparked hope within us and then left too soon to decide if they had ever even existed. Regardless, he continues to remain my father's favorite employee, mostly because of his loyalty to Vex, including its authentic booze, but also because he keeps a Tommy gun underneath the bar and is not afraid to use it.

"I'll have a bourbon ... make that two," I say.

"Oh, I don't usually drink," Luther says nervously.

"It's not for you," I reply as I purse my lips. Jack laughs.

"Alice drinks more than any man I've ever seen," he says. I wink at Jack as he hands me my drinks.

Luther looks as though he disapproves. I down my first drink, letting my head fall back a little while I absorb all the pleasure that could ever be held within a glass. A few moments later, I notice Luther staring at me as though I'm insane. Ignoring him, I focus on downing my second drink. I can feel the alcohol being absorbed in my body, slowly reaching my head, causing the music to seem to grow softer and my senses to dull. That was my favorite part about it all. The world vanished and nobody was anywhere except where they were at that very moment. Any lingering thoughts were void and I was filled with only a sense of pleasure.

Luther places his hand on my back, a worrisome expression spreading over his face. I allow him to lead me out of the club, leaning against him so I don't fall. I glance back once more before leaving and, even through all the smoke and rummaging bodies, I spot Jack shaking his head. He knows me too well.

Luther pushes the large wooden door open and I feel a rush of cold air hit my body as I stumble out into the street. It would be impossible to ignore the full moon above as it beats down powerfully on us, enchanting us with her light. The moon's love is the only love I have any recollection of receiving since childhood. A memory of my four-year-old self flashes through my conscience in her oversized white nightgown, standing by the window on her tiptoes, desperately trying to catch a glimpse of the moon before drifting off to sleep. I've always believed the moon watched over me, keeping me safe while my father was out burying gentlemen who refused to be as corrupt as he was.

"Alice, where do you live? I'll escort you home."

I had almost forgotten his presence.

"You don't want to go there. Nobody does." My house is filled only with loneliness, and the thought of it seems too discomforting at the current moment.

"Fine. Let's go." His voice is rough, clearly upset with my refusal to answer his question.

I prefer him this way, hostility in men being one of my favorite characteristics. His arm is still around my waist as we walk through the French Quarter past a homeless man spitting his teeth out in the street and the sound of gunshots in the distance. Luther flinches beside me but I remain unaffected. This is how it is for us in New Orleans: it's the city of the night, the haunted city. Sometimes I get so enveloped in it, I feel like I've been swallowed whole by a beast.

We reach a large brownstone building with coliseum-like verandas built on each side. He ushers me up the stairs swiftly, his eyes searching the premises anxiously as he fidgets with his keys before unlocking the door. His place is small and dusty with not much but an old velvet couch and a disintegrating rug. Out of the corner of my eye, I spot the powder room and excuse myself, scurrying down the hall and slamming the door behind me. I'm parched and my stomach is growling, begging for more. I pull a flask out of my stockings, my secret stash. I could tell Luther would be opposed to me furthering my state of intoxication and I was in no mood to argue. I unscrew the cap with my teeth and ravenously gulp down the remaining amount of gin, letting it trickle down my throat and onto my dress. My mind begins to spin and my thoughts float all around the room, leaving me paralyzed. My flask slips from my fingertips and the sound of the metal hitting the floor rings in my ears for several moments. I feel as though I'm falling, but my body is numb, leaving my eyes as the only witness to my crashing body. The last thing I can recall is Luther's voice in the distance asking if I'm alright. Then everything goes dark.

II

I WAKE up with my hip bones digging into the wood floor. I wish I could say these sorts of things didn't happen often, but I won't lie. I use my right hand to steady myself as I crawl up onto a velvet seat. I look down at my body. Blood runs down my chest and my dress is torn down the side, leaving threads unraveling around my waist.

I look for signs of a wound as I notice my toes stuck in dried blood. I've accumulated plenty of wounds from my countless nights of intoxication. Oddly enough, I don't spot any. I also don't feel any pain.

Rising to my feet, I catch a glimpse of myself in the hall mirror. My golden blonde hair is sticking up in all directions, my eyeliner is smudged down to my cheeks, and my eyes are bloodshot and frantic. The curse of drinking causes me to once again awaken to someone unrecognizable in the mirror.

I smell a stench that I cannot make out. It's a vile scent and, though it's familiar, I cannot figure out where I know it from. I turn my head, noticing a pool of blood near the bathroom door. My heart's beating out of my chest. I know what I'm going to find, but I'm desperately hoping I don't.

I dodge past the blood and with the tips of my fingers gently push the bathroom door open. The door creaks and as my eyes make their way down to the floor, I gasp. Blood seems to fill up the whole room, splattered on the mirror, sink, and top of the toilet.

Luther lies on the floor in a disturbing position. A butcher knife is thrust through his chest, his neck curved in an unnatural way, leaving his left collar bone popping out. His eyes remain open and pierced with shock, so dilated I can almost see my reflection in his pupils. His dressing shirt was so red you would never know that it had once been fine white.

I'm motionless for what seems like eternity, unable to tear my eyes away from his limp body. I steady my breath and, in meek movements, slowly back away into the hallway. I feel my back hit the wall and my body begins to sink to the floor. Suddenly, memories flash through my mind of me stabbing Luther multiple times and ripping his eyes out with my nails.

I'm immoral and vicious at times, but never monstrous. What have I done? A voice in the back of my mind screams at me to flee, that it's only a matter of time before someone notices that he's missing. It takes all my might to gather myself up and leave the crime scene.

I dash to the bedroom and raid Luther's closet, throwing on an oversized dinner jacket to hide the blood that's drenched all over me. I peek out the window to make sure no passersby see me leave his place, before sprinting as fast as my feet will take me. I'm in such a frenzy that I don't even realize I'm heading back to Vex.

When I reach the club, it's empty. In the daylight hours, Vex is just a dirty old bank. The wallpaper's chipped and the floors reek of spilt alcohol. I stumble up the spiral staircase leading to my father's office. The door's half open and my father is hovering over his desk, drink in hand, reading the Sunday paper. He's large and has dark hair and green eyes. The infamous gangster Benjamin W. possesses a lion-like quality. It enables him to walk into any room and immediately all other occupants cower a bit in his presence—even myself at times, though I never let him know that. His eyes dart up to see me breathing heavily, standing at the threshold of the door.

"What's happened?" His voice is loud and deep, echoing throughout the room.

"I ... I did something foolish." I attempt to steady my voice but feel the panic overtake me.

"Alice, I'm working. I don't have time for your games."

"It's not a game!" I cry out. "There's a boy and he's dead ... please, I need your help!"

He does not look startled, though with my past I cannot expect him to. He merely sets his drink down, displeased.

"Where is he?" he growls.

III

Approximately an hour later, my father and his men are gathered outside Luther's building, appearing more than slightly suspicious. I'm at the corner, lurking by the alley that reeks of piss and fumes. I cough at the stench. I'm too traumatized to get near his body, especially knowing that I'm the reason for his current state.

I watch as the men walk in and out of the building casually. Seeing dead bodies is nothing new for them. In fact, this is one of the rare occasions when they have to clean up a mess that isn't theirs. I imagine them all in there right now, my father probably looking over Luther's body, screeching orders at his men to make sure to not miss a single drop of blood. The house would have to be properly sanitized to avoid any room for an investigation, not that one would even take place. My father regularly dines with the chief of police and has most of the department paid off already.

I watch as Victor, my father's right-hand man, adjusts his hat as he lights up a cigarette with a sly expression on his face. I creep further back into the alley and wait there for a while, wishing I'd remembered to refill my flask before I left Vex. Time passes too slowly without booze.

I hear a loud sound and my father's men rush out of the building and speed away in their automobiles. Two men pass by the alley and I hear one say, "That guy was a close call. Glad Victor came in when he did."

Wondering what he meant by that, I steal one last glance at Luther's building before I wander off down the opposite street.

IV

Two nights later, I'm back at Vex sitting by the bar, a glass of whiskey in my hand. My eyes are fixed on the large wooden clock hanging above me. My eyes follow the little hand as each second it strikes another number, wondering how time was invented. It's the strangest concept to me. Once, when I was little, I put my father's pocket watch in the freezer so I could stop time. He laughed at my foolishness in a repulsive tone as he reached down with his large hands, picking me up from my waist and throwing me in my bedroom. I still remember the sound of the lock clicking shut. He left me there for two days.

"Alice, your drink?"

I smile before I even look up. Jack's got on a white, collared shirt with his black tie hanging loosely around his neck. He places a glass of whiskey, my third one so far today, in front of me. I blow him a kiss and he laughs. I hear the door open and a tall figure rushes in toward us. He is quick, lanky, and sets his hands against the bar, practically digging his filthy fingernails into the wood. He looks familiar. I can almost smell it.

"Could I get a bourbon please?" His voice is hoarse and he remains standing, impatiently eyeing the room.

My eyes are focused on the floor. I brush my hair behind my left ear so I can listen. I hear Jack shuffling through bottles and clinking glasses as he pours his drink, setting it in front of him.

"Hey, look, my brother's dead and I'm pretty sure he was here a few nights ago. I found a matchbox from your bar on his floor. You happen to know who he was with?" His voice is loud and intense. His eyes are rageful. Jack shakes his head.

So, this must be Luther's brother.

"No, sir. A lot of people pass through here and no one is going to remember them unless they are especially unusual."

"Well, I happen to know he was here and he was murdered the same night. I saw the damn crime scene myself before I was knocked out by someone. Convenient for them, I didn't see the damn son of a bitch!" He raises his hands making crazy hand gestures and almost baring his teeth in saliva. A few of the bystanders begin to shoot glances over at him. He doesn't seem to notice as he continues on his rant. "He got me on the back of my head and by the time I woke up my brother's body had disappeared along with the pools of blood left around his place!"

"Look man," Jack replies, trying to keep himself collected. "I don't know what the hell you're talking about and I think you need to quiet down or get the hell out of here."

Luther's brother takes one last swig of his drink before smashing it on the floor and walking out in a scoff. The sound of broken glass shattering lingers in the air for a few moments after. I can feel the anxiety rising in my veins. I'd anticipated his family or friends might come after him, but the look in his brother's eyes showed he was out for blood. The notion that I had been the one to kill Luther was still too much for me to bear. I needed to get him as far away from finding out the truth as possible. I had to take action, and soon, before my father found out about this. I know my father would just kill him if he found out that Luther had a brother who existed. Especially one with a vitality such as this. The truth was I felt too guilty for killing Luther. The thought of his brother having to die too was too evil, even for me. If I led him astray, no one else would have to suffer because of what I'd done.

I dash out of the bar, hoping to catch him before he disappears out into the chaos of the city. I run down Bienville Street, trying to spot him. Nothing. I take another turn and run head smack into him.

"Watch it," he growls at me.

I stand in front of him. He's wearing a black button-down, navy velvet waistcoat, dark slacks, and a coat which sweeps the floor. Even with his striking features, so similar to his brother's, his skin seems more rough, dirty even. His blond hair is messy and cut shorter than Luther's and his eyes resemble dark holes shot through his head. I remain silent for a few moments, not sure exactly what to say or how to get in his head.

It's strange, I'm usually very good at reading people. I'm almost never speechless. I can count on my fingers the number of times I've been in a bind I couldn't talk myself out of or found a man who got under my skin. Most of those times have been with my father and he never lets me forget it.

"I heard what you said back there in the bar ... about your brother." It was all I managed to get out.

"Yeah, it's a goddamn tragedy, that's what it is." He spits on the street as he reaches into his coat pocket and pulls out his cigarette case. He lights up a smoke as he continues. "This city's hell if there ever was one. My brother was the only person I ever had. He was uncorrupted." He didn't seem sad, only angry. I suppose they are often emotions entwined in one another, the anger taking over so the sadness wouldn't.

I think of how Luther had only been looking out for my safety. I hadn't known him at all and yet, in the short time I'd been around him, it was obvious he had been a gentleman—and it is not often you see those here. To think that I was the one to take him away made my heart clench. I shake off those thoughts as soon as they come. I was in a drunken rage when I killed him. That isn't who I truly am. Guilt floods my entire body, making me feel as though I would become physically sick. I reach into my stocking, retrieving my antiquated metal flask and taking an awfully long sip of gin.

"You seem young to drink," he says, studying me. He looks as though he can't be that much older than I.

"And you seem foolish to go after a murderer," I reply, my voice bordering on harsh. He smirks as he takes another drag of his cigarette before extending his hand.

"I think I forgot to mention, I'm Kyle." I cautiously shake his hand, our fingertips meeting. His skin is as rough as I'd anticipated it would be. Cold as well, oddly cold.

"I'm Alice," I say. He nods in acknowledgement.

"I think I can help you." I try to sound as cool as possible.

"How so?" He sounds unconvinced.

"Well, you know, I spend a lot of time at Vex. I know almost everyone who goes there. I could help you investigate."

Truthfully, I wasn't friendly at all with anyone who went to my father's club. I knew of their names or faces but hardly ever spoke to them. They didn't know much about me either. Most of them knew me for two things: being Benjamin's daughter and causing havoc almost everywhere I go. That was all.

He raises an eyebrow. "Well … I suppose I could use some assistance."

I try my best to hide my feelings of triumph. It was easier than I'd anticipated, but you see, that's the thing with men. They're too easy to manipulate. It almost makes me feel bad for them. Almost.

"I would say we should start at the club, but after your recent behavior, that might not be the wisest decision."

He scoffs at me.

"How about the crime scene? We could go searching for evidence," I propose.

He shakes his head. "Those bums knocked me out and had the place spotless by the time I woke up … except for this." He looks both ways down the street as though he possesses something of value that must be held with the utmost importance. Then, he reaches into his coat pocket and pulls out a handkerchief. It is beige with lace trim. Vintage, no doubt. It has dark red bloodstains on the ends and the initials E.W.

I knew it, of course, because it belonged to me. Well, it was my mother's once, but I kept it as a keepsake after her passing. I went no place without it on me somewhere. I usually kept it around my waist or pinned to the inside of my dress. I kept a straight face, nodding and pretending to look fascinated as I examined it.

"Where did you find it?"

"In the living room under the rug." A memory of me leaning down to feel the rug flashes through my mind.

"Do you suppose it's his blood or the killer's?" I cursed myself for being so careless. How could I not think to make sure I had all my belongings before I left. Now, not only did Kyle hold crucial evidence connecting me to the murder but I'd lost the only remaining item I had that belonged to my mother.

"I hope it's the killer's. That way, when I find the son of a bitch, I can shove it down his throat and make him choke on it."

His vulgarity and passion were enticing. I found myself both fascinated and terrified by his twisted fantasies, wondering what else he was conspiring.

"What would you use? A knife?" I suggest sarcastically. I wasn't sure if he hadn't caught my sarcasm or if he was simply choosing to ignore it, but the tone of his voice suddenly became serious.

"Oh, I'd come with a few devices. Stab him a few times in the ribs, bash his head in with a hammer and then, right when he can't bear the pain any longer, I'd pick out his teeth one by one." He stared into my eyes in an invasive way as he spoke. It was as though the entire city and street and every sound around us vanished. For a few moments, I lost my grasp on reality, feeling hypnotized by his eyes and his rage.

"Beautiful," I reply finally. He tears his eyes away from mine and nods his head as though he's satisfied with himself. It's getting dark now, the night sky caving in on us, making me want to escape from him and never leave all at once. The city is beautiful in its own sick way—similar to how we are, I suppose.

"I've got to get going. Meet me on the corner of Bienville and Treme at noon tomorrow and we'll devise a plan."

"Alright, see you then Alice."

I whip around and walk back down the street before I have time to digest the last moments of our encounter. Being around Kyle made me feel out of control. He's powerful and intrusive and it's as though I have to struggle to be able to just be around him. He's vicious and so am I and people of our kind aren't supposed to meet one another. It reminded me of how my father used to say that humans were divided into two categories, predator and prey, just as animals are. He always emphasized how important it was to be a predator and that being weak was about the worst thing in the world a man could ever become. Kyle was certainly a predator, but not like the others I had seen. There was something different about him that I couldn't quite describe, and as I walked down the streets returning home, I wondered how I would ever defeat him.

V

I WAKE up the next morning with the light streaming in through my windows. I stumble out of bed and reach for my bottle of gin at the edge of my bedside table. I can't wake up without my medicine. The day gets better the moment I feel the liquid burning in my throat. I light up a smoke as I examine my surroundings.

My bedroom is a large space with two European-style windows opening to the balcony. I keep them open almost at all times, my thin withering curtains strung across the ceiling. My beige satin sheets are tangled up in my comforter. The headboard to my bed is broken straight through the middle, leaving my mattress leaning to one side. My bed creaks incessantly due to the broken springs in my mattress. An assortment of slips, drop-waists, garters, stockings, loose-fitting blouses, bloomers, and pearls lay flung out across the wooden floors.

This is my mess and I keep it just this way. I'll never fold my clothing neatly or make up my bed in the morning. I've just never been that way, never will be. And if I am, I hope I get shot to hell. I glide toward the balcony wearing only an oversized dressing shirt and my beige stockings. My once clean stockings were now dirt-stricken from my late-night pacing around on the balcony.

Smoking and people-watching were my favorite late-night activities. I would crawl down on my knees and hang my legs off the side of the ledge. In the dark, the occasional onlooker would only notice what looked like a shadow smoking in the distance. Most people never bother to look up though. It's bewildering really how people are so caught up in any number of dramas and misfortunes that they miss outrageous moments and details such as this. And those missed moments are typically the most amusing. I've spent many hours out on this balcony playing the shadow and eavesdropping on everyone from bureaucrats to bums. In the end, they're all the same: lonely, inadequate and yearning for more. More of any and every materialistic fantasy they have constructed in their minds that they conclude will lead to their happiness. I wish they knew what a waste of time it all was. I wish they could perceive life the way I do: an endless parade of madness and distress with only the smallest of joys in between.

I exhale as my eyes search over the rows of daunting old Southern homes and fume-filled streets. I glance back at the clock on my bedside table and realize I'm late to meet Kyle. I throw on my black bloomers underneath my dressing shirt and my beat-up Mary Janes. I dash down the stairs past my father's room. I stop in front of it, considering if I should say good morning to him. I shake my head. He hates to be disturbed and especially after the mess he and his men had to clean up.

To my father, I was a headache, a consistent issue. I drank too much, slept with too many men, spoke my opinions too loud, and never did what I was told. I lingered for a moment, my eyes going over the light brown wood and the glass doorknob, feeling like I was eight years old again, pacing back and forth in front of my father's bedroom, waiting for him to notice me. When he would, it would usually result in him slamming the door in my face and telling me to go to bed.

Even then, he hated me. Maybe he always knew I was trouble. I used to think it was because he missed my mother—though, contrary to that argument, he's had countless women and affairs with every youthful beauty in sight. He's as infamous for being cold-hearted as he is for being a gangster. I suppose that makes him hypocritical for criticizing my romantic affairs. But what did he expect? He made me this way.

The only times I've ever made my father proud were when I showed an exceptional amount of heartlessness. When he taught me how to shoot a gun, I had impeccable aim and his face lit up with approval. But when he put a rat in front of me, I refused to shoot it. I could never kill animals—it's too sick. Even being raised in his world, I'm still occasionally caught off guard and let my emotions rule me.

I was seven the first time I saw a dead body. My father had brought me down to the tunnels where his men would smuggle liquor into the club. We had crawled down through the street entrance. The walls were dripping with sewage and it reeked of cheap liquor. By the time my father and I arrived, Victor had a gun pointed to a man's head. I never saw what the man's face looked like, but I remember he had a limp and wild, curly brown hair shooting up in all directions. He was weeping and begging for mercy at the hands of Victor. Victor didn't even flinch as he shot him in the back of the head. The man's body fell flat into the muddy water. His skull was open and I could see parts of his brain oozing out. I hid behind my father, afraid the man would somehow come back to life and shove bits of his brain down my throat.

"Don't be afraid, Alice. This is how we deal with problems. We take them out. This way, they don't come back. You understand?"

I nodded, not understanding what most things meant when I was seven.

I come back to reality, catching my breath and continuing down the stairs. I rush out into the street past the usual thieves and mothers with their children wrapped safely in their carriages. I make it to the corner of Bienville and Treme, where I told Kyle to meet me. He couldn't meet me at Vex for fear of my father or his men lurking around overhearing our conversation.

If my father knew, I couldn't imagine what he'd do to Kyle—or to myself for being so foolish.

I could feel the aching in my chest every time I thought about the words coming out of Kyle's mouth yesterday. I was up all night, tossing and turning, unable to get his voice out of my head. I've had night terrors for most of my life. In some, my body is frozen but my mind is awake as ever. It's horrifying because I'm watching demons and entities standing at the foot of my bed taunting me. Without any control of my body, I'm forced to watch them until they decide they're done with me.

I see Kyle walking toward me. In the daylight hours, the sun seems to shun him, gleaming light on the filthy street and in every corner except for the ones he passes. He's wearing an oversized brown coat unbuttoned, revealing his dark underlayers. His large boots reach his calves and his hair looks unwashed and stale. He continues to walk closer, his brows furrowing, betraying his obvious irritation.

"God, this fucking city. Even just on my walk over, I almost got mugged," he scoffs.

I nod. "Just another day in paradise."

He laughs and shrugs his coat off a bit, letting his dressing shirt stick out. I can't help but stare at the nape of his bare neck and how it leads impeccably well to his jawline and the cut of his cheekbones. As my eyes pass over him, I spot Victor out of the corner of my eye. In a panic, I throw my arms around Kyle, digging my nails into his back and pulling him around the corner so we're hidden from Victor's view. He shrieks out in pain midway between the two streets. I let him go and his back hits up against the brick wall. His body makes a thud as I hear his back bones meet the brick. We're both breathing heavily, my mind racing with paranoia, waiting for Victor to appear and chaos to strike. He doesn't.

"What the hell was that for?" Kyle takes a step toward me, his warm breath on my neck.

"Nothing, sorry," I say, not bothering to fabricate a story. I was too relieved we hadn't been caught.

"Are you always like this?" he says, adjusting his coat.

"Always," I respond, as I begin walking down the street, hoping to further the distance between us and Victor. Kyle's annoyance is apparent, yet he follows me nonetheless. We come in view of the St. Louis Cemetery. Memories of myself as a child flood my mind. I'd leave flowers at my mother's grave every Friday. My father never came with me. When I was younger, I assumed it was because he was too grief-stricken. I know now it was because he was angry at her for leaving us so soon. I have no memories of my father and mother in love, but a few years back I found a letter he had written her. In it, he confessed his love to her and told her she made him want to live on even at his darkest moments. I was shocked that my father could ever show affection, much less be romantic. I never told him that I'd found it, of course, but it was a sign he was human, and that alone was enough for me.

Kyle nudges me.

"What?" I respond.

"You do that often?"

"I'm not sure I know what you're implying," I reply.

"Doze off that way. What were you thinking of?" His eyes peer into mine with a mix of curiosity and suspicion.

"I was thinking how much I despise this cemetery." The opposite was true. It's my favorite one in the city.

"Well, you shouldn't. It's my favorite one."

A small smile forms on my lips at his reaction, but I don't dare let him see it. He forces the gate open, the metal creaking as we slip quietly inside. The tombstones and mausoleums are practically ancient. It's a wonder that they managed to survive all these years. It seems as though the older they were, the more beautiful they became, as did the personality each one seemed to carry. I have never left this city, but I couldn't imagine any cemetery in the world could hold more tragedy or spirits than this one. I hoped one day my corpse would be lucky enough to call this home.

"If you listen closely you can almost hear them," Kyle says apprehensively, his eyes examining the tombs.

"Hear who?"

"The spirits who reside here." I raise my eyebrows at him, unsure if he's attempting to be comical.

"Yes, and I suppose we should ask the Voodoo spirits for a favor. Maybe they'll know who killed your brother."

"Don't be silly. Only Lucifer would know that." He was clearly ignoring my sarcasm.

"And why is that? Because anyone who's ever committed a crime must belong to him?"

"No, not just any crime ... you didn't see the way I found him." His face darkens, as does any sarcasm left in his voice. I could feel my heart beginning to pound in my chest, my mind desperately trying to suppress the repulsive memories of his brother's deceased body. Kyle's eyes seem to wander off, the memories haunting him.

"He was killed with a butcher knife. A damn butcher knife, can you believe that? From the looks of the wounds all over his body, you'd have to assume he'd been stabbed at least a dozen times."

He shakes his head in disgust. He's more miserable than I am, which is something I never deemed possible. "Have you ever seen a dead body?"

"Haven't we all?" I reply, struggling to keep my cool demeanor.

"Yes, I suppose we have, living in a city like this."

"I still don't understand what that has to do with Lucifer."

"A man that demented surely couldn't have just come from anywhere. He had to have been born with some otherworldly evil inside him. Would you disagree?"

I wondered if he was right; maybe I was evil. How far could one go before the line that one could return from had far been surpassed?

"No, I don't think anyone would dare disagree with that."

"I thought you knew how to investigate," he says, changing the subject abruptly.

"Well it's not as if you have any clues where to begin, seeing as the only evidence you've attained is some old handkerchief." One which I must steal back somehow.

"My brother worked at the docks. We should begin there, see if anyone there knows how he came to be at Vex in the first place." I nod and we begin walking toward the inner city.

"Yes, possibly to meet a friend," I say, attempting to plant an idea in his head that it must have been someone Luther knew prior.

"Exactly. My brother's a good kid. He's not the type to be seen roaming around in speakeasies or going against the law." I would have laughed at the idiocy if I hadn't met his brother. Luther certainly had been a prude. "He must have been meeting someone of significance."

"It's possible," I reply apathetically. His eyebrows furrow as he seems disappointed in my lack of interest in his remarks.

The only interest I have at the moment is increasing my gin intake. "Hold on." I halt in the middle of the street and carefully slide my hand into my stocking to retrieve my flask. I rip the lid cap off, violently gulping down the burning liquid. Kyle merely watches me while I hungrily drain every last drop.

"How much do you need?" he says as he grabs my wrist, pulling me forward.

"More still," I say.

I expect him to let go but he does not. We continue walking through the streets, hand and hand, our eyes not meeting, both of us consumed in our thoughts, navigating through the harsh, demented city that we call home. This is as good as it gets in New Orleans. You've got to hold onto any companionship you may find, though I would not dare call Kyle a companion.

We wander through the city as it erupts with pseudo-psychics and street performers amongst the shop owners and high-class women in fur coats. One woman has on a fitting, turquoise Victorian gown that reaches the floor and drags behind her, accumulating the grime from the street. She echoes wealth and boredom. I imagine her wed to a corrupt politician, her days filled with dinner parties she would rather not attend and conversations containing only trifling issues. Perhaps she had once dreamt of running off to live in the country, spending her days riding horses and caring for lambs. But dreams are dreams, and now she lives as she's told, as her rational mind says she should. This could be completely untrue of course, yet I often love to give stories to strangers, if only to make the world seem a little less awful.

A man walking in a frenzy bumps into Kyle, throwing him off step, causing our hands to break apart and our eyes to meet briefly as if we had both lost something that we couldn't decipher.

"It's right up this way." His voice is serious. He's once again back to being a brute.

"Lead the way," I reply.

The docks are beyond grotesque, steamboats lined up as far as the eye can see, the pollution from them looming over us as clouds would. Men swarm all around us, carrying cargo that came from up the Mississippi. Kyle approaches a man wearing dark brown slacks, a white-and-black striped shirt, and black overalls attached to his belt. He looks filthy and worn down, sweat dripping from his forehead.

"Excuse me, do you work here?"

"Yes, sir. I do."

"My brother worked here as well. His name was Luther. Did you know him?"

The man furrows his brows and looks around, as if trying to put the name to a body.

"Sounds familiar. He might have worked the graveyard shift with me once. He's a tall, lanky fellow, yeah? Real quiet, works hard."

"Yeah, that's him," Kyle says surely.

"Would there happen to be anyone around who could provide us with more information about his schedule, perhaps?" I say, interjecting. The man contemplates for a moment.

"John. He's up on the ship at the moment, unloading."

"Thank you." I snatch Kyle's hand and take charge, striding down the wooden dock, my heels clicking as I go. The uncleanly environment blended with the view of the Mississippi creates an almost ghostly atmosphere. The men unload cargo in robotic movements with grim faces and woeful eyes. One man appears to be shouting demands at the rest. He's the largest man in sight, dressed to the socks in dark layers, his body language emanating power. This man was a predator, as my father would say. I proceed to tap him on the shoulder, and as he turns around, a hard expression is already glued to his face.

"Who are you?" He talks down to me, his voice ringing with irritation.

"I'm Alice. This is Kyle," I say bravely. I raise my chin high and stand on my tiptoes just a bit. "We were wondering about one of your workers. Luther."

A look of recognition passes over his face.

"Yes, he worked for me."

"Worked?" I remark. He hesitates before Kyle interrupts him.

"When was the last time you saw him?" Kyle asks.

"Last week. He was scheduled to work yesterday but didn't come."

The docks are vital, shipments coming in day and night at any given hour. If one man is absent, an entire shipment could be at risk of being delayed. He should be furious that Luther's been away. He should be demanding to know where he is, yet he is acting as though it's hardly an inconvenience. My father has all his alcohol smuggled and imported through these docks. If it's late, it could cause a night at Vex to be in a drought and the penalties for delays are harsh to say the least.

"What shipments are you in charge of?"

"Canned goods, fabrics, machinery mostly." He's lying through his teeth.

"Alcohol?" Kyle suggests aggressively. Kyle has passion and anger, but lacks the ability to hide his motives, and his inability to interrogate properly was unnerving. John's lips purse and his voice becomes reluctant.

"No. I don't take part in those kinds of transactions. I'm a decent, honest man trying to make a living. Now, I've wasted too much of my time already answering these ridiculous questions. You kids run along now." I give Kyle an irritated look as I pull him by the sleeve, dragging him to the far side of the ship to escape John's view. When we reach a far enough distance away, I grab

Kyle, viciously pinning him against a wooden door.

“Alcohol?” I mimic his voice. “Are you an imbecile?”

“That man is a liar. You think nothing suspicious goes on at the docks?”

“No, but you’ve just ruined any chance of us reeling information out of him! Haven’t you ever heard of discretion?” I’m practically growling now, my voice low and rage pulsing through my veins. He laughs wickedly as though he’s almost enjoying it.

“Alice, you aren’t like anyone.”

I ignore his comment, instead proceeding to shove palms against his chest, causing the doorjamb behind him to break open and send Kyle crashing backward onto the floor. Dust clouds my eyes and throat, causing me to cough frantically. As the dust seems to settle, I carefully open my eyes to examine the room. It’s a small, wooden office: a desk, chair, no windows, and complete with a large door. Papers flood the small table, stacks piled neatly on one another. A lamp sits next to the desk, shedding light on the papers. Kyle picks himself up from the floor, brushing the dust off his coat.

“I’m done with your temper tantrums.” His teeth are out, heaving. I ignore him and walk over to the desk. The stacks of paper seem to be files. I sift through them.

“What are those?” Kyle asks. He stays put across the room.

“Looks like files, paperwork from business deals. Companies they work with.”

Kyle nods. “Which ones?”

“Williams Corp., S&W, Dawson Brothers. Nothing out of the ordinary.”

“Let me look.”

I walk toward the door and peer out, hoping no one heard the fall Kyle just took. Not a figure in sight. I make a mental note that it was good we were right next to the ladder, in case we were to be caught—an easy escape route—or, we could jump in the river, but that was always a drag.

"Hey, look at this." Kyle hands me a paper that shows transactions with a company called V's Apothecary.

"I know this place. It's a shop off Chartres Street." I'd never actually been inside, but I'd passed by it several times and it always gave me the chills. The curtains were always drawn and I'd never seen anyone go inside.

"It's strange … All the companies they deal with are large manufacturers and then they give shipments to a single shop? Something's off."

"Something's always off," I mutter, shoving the paper back on the stack, adjusting it to leave no trace that anyone had been here.

"Come on. Let's go before we're caught." I creep toward the door and we sneak out quietly, returning to the main streets. Darkness fills the sky, leaving only glimpses of the day behind. Kyle stands beside me, lost in thought.

"Look at them. They're insane," he says, motioning to the world around us.

The city is buzzing, each person rushing past one another, arguments brewing between the locals, and bums sleeping on sidewalks as comfortably as one would at home in bed.

"And we are sane?"

"No, we are worse."

"I agree."

"You do?" He turns toward me, genuinely surprised that I had agreed with him.

"Yes, we are far worse, because we know better. We can see it, yet we choose to partake in it. They, on the other hand, are blind to it."

He looks stunned.

"Exactly. How the hell are we gonna figure this out?" His voice sounds defeated.

"We will," I say assuredly as I place my hand on his shoulder.

"I just can't let my brother die this way. I have to get justice for him." His voice is hoarse, his eyes are wet. "I have to find out who did it. I need them to suffer as greatly as he did, feel the pain of a thousand knives in their chest, and the look..."

"The look?" I ask.

"Yes. The look in his eyes when he sees that I am the one to bring him to his end. The moment he realizes I'll be the last person he ever encounters. And when I know he is taking his final breath, I'll smile. I'll smile with all my teeth and soak in all the beauty of revenge. All the sweet damn beauty."

I swallow and let my eyes lower to the pavement. This is what he craves to do to me. Craves more than anything in the world. It was strange being so near to someone who has a hatred for you, and even more strange when they are incognizant of it. This is what he will do to me if he finds out. It takes all my might to respond.

"Well then, we better find the son of a bitch."

VI

THE next day, I'm sitting in my father's office while he's yelling at one of his men over the telephone. My legs are crossed. I'm wearing my emerald green dress which barely reaches past my knees and has velvet buttons down to my waist and a thin sash draped across my hips. My pearls are strung around my neck loosely, falling to my ribs. I'm pretending to read the newspaper while lounging on the dark velvet love seat.

"What do you mean it's coming tomorrow? I said tonight! By midnight or I'll go down there and get it my goddamn self!" My father slams the phone frantically down, rattling his desk. I look up at him, my eyebrows raised.

"What now, Alice?"

"I didn't say anything," I say flatly.

"Are you just gonna sit there looking pretty? Make yourself useful and go down and tell Victor I need him." He adjusts his tie as he picks up the phone and begins yelling again.

I scowl as I rise from the love seat and adjust my pearls. I walk down the spiral staircase and spot Victor at the bar. He's not drinking, of course. He never drinks on the job. He takes being my father's right hand extremely seriously. He's got eyes like a hawk and he moves quickly. Nothing gets past Victor. Trust me, I've tried. He can't be bought either. I've never seen anyone so loyal; he would take a bullet for my father. It stuns me how many men look up to my father. Yes, he owns a speakeasy and maintains an unsurpassed reputation for being untouchable, but on the inside he's nothing but a lonesome, livid man. None of his women care for him, his men abide out of fear, not respect, and his only daughter is nothing but an inconvenience to him. In my eyes, a homeless beggar has more to live for.

"Victor, my father needs you," I call out to him mundanely.

Within seconds, he's racing up the stairs. I walk through the club, past the jazz band practicing their vocals and mobsters playing cards. I push open the doors to Vex, out into the raging day, straight into the lion's den: V's Apothecary.

VII

THE shop is just as I remembered it. Dark, dusty, and easily unnoticed by the average onlooker. It doesn't strike me as completely odd to choose a place such as this for illegal activity. It's hiding in plain sight. Most illegal activity took to underground tunnels or abandoned real estate. A mystical shop was a new approach, I'll give them that.

I swing open the shop door and bells ring as I enter. Cabinets line the walls, filled with jars full of herbs and oils. Adjacent to those are shelves filled with books, which I presume have to do with herbal medicine and the magical properties of herbs.

Marie Laveau is greatly known throughout the city, many going to her grave to bring her gifts in hopes she may fulfill their wishes. My father called it one of the devil's many games, which only made me want to play it even more.

My father is by no means a godly man. In truth, I just believe he's afraid of the otherworldly. I don't believe in God myself. If there is a God, I don't want anything to do with him.

I see Kyle has arrived before me. I spot him throwing his hands in the air, interrogating the shopkeeper. The old woman looks so frightened. Kyle towers over her, speaking in a rough manner. I rush over to them and get a better look at the keeper. She's small, pale skin like a doll, and these large, round eyes. She's wearing her hair up in a neatly-fixed bun and her spectacles are gold-rimmed around the edges. She's dressed awfully out of this decade. She's wearing a corset, for Christ's sake. Her gown is dark blue with layers of skirts underneath her corset. She reminds me of a mouse, whimpering and cowering in fear under him.

"Kyle!" I shout at him. He notices my presence. The tension between them eases as he calms himself.

"My apologies. My friend here is unwell and isn't acting like himself." Kyle bites his bottom lip and turns his gaze away.

"It ... it's alright... I'm confused at what the young gentleman is referring to." I whip my head around, glaring at Kyle viciously.

"Men can be so malevolent," I say.

"Coming from—"

I cut him off without even batting an eyelash. I step in front of him, steering the conversation my way. His dissonant attitude would just not do.

"Needless to say, we are just too curious about this shop. It's ... quite unconventional," I say, my eyes gazing over a jar which holds a tentacle inside of it.

"Well ... we have an array of herbs, oils, remarkable mixtures, you know."

"I've heard," I say, nodding and pretending to look fascinated.

"We also have dozens of books on natural plant remedies and elixirs for certain kinds of illness."

"Where do your herbs come from?" A perplexed look spreads across her face, so I continue on. "Anything you receive from out of the state ... or from across the water, perhaps?" She looks pensive for a moment.

"No, no ... the owner of the shop is very particular. Everything must be authentic. Most of it comes from her heritage." She lowers her voice and looks around as she whispers, "You know, she's a descendent of Marie Laveau herself."

Now that was interesting. I'd always found the Voodoo queen to be quite intriguing.

"Do you think you could arrange a meeting? I'd love to speak to her personally." The lady nods her head.

"Yes. She's in the back right now. She does tarot readings during the afternoons." I nod as the lady motions to a doorway draped closed with dark velvet curtains. She pushes back the curtains, revealing a thin woman with beautifully curly hair seated at a round table. Her eyes were closed and her hands lay on a deck of cards spread across the table.

"Beatrice," the lady calls softly to her. Beatrice's eyes flick open. She's strikingly beautiful, the kind that one does not see often. Her eyes wander my figure and pass over to Kyle, who stands a few feet behind me.

"Hello." Her lips part as she motions for us to come closer.

"How do you do?" I ask respectfully as I take the seat next to her.

"Well. Even more so now."

Kyle doesn't speak a word, thank God. He has no manners or care for niceties. To think he was going to investigate Luther's murder alone is beyond comical. I may be the daughter of a gangster, but my father raised me with manners. I can hear his voice in my head ringing, "If you are gonna take a fellow for everything he's worth, you might as well have the common decency to ask how his day is." I clear my throat.

"We are in search of answers, and our search has led us to you." Beatrice raises her eyebrows.

"And what sort of search may that be?"

"There's been a terrible tragedy. Kyle's" — I motion to him — "brother has been murdered. And we have reason to believe it may have been work-affiliated." She remains composed, the word murder seeming to have no effect on her. I continue, "Do you receive merchandise from overseas, by chance? Or does a man named John sound familiar?" Her eyes light up with recognition yet she does not speak. She simply gathers the deck in front of her and begins shuffling, her long fingernails grasping the cards ever so carefully. She places them in a triangular pattern, turning each one over. The first card reveals a skull and crossbones, the following is what seems to be a tower or castle of sorts, and the final card is a man who hangs upside down. She taps her fingers on the table, her expression seeming to shift.

"You don't truly want me to answer your question, do you?" Her eyes lock with mine as if she and I share a secret which no one else in the world knows.

"Why would you say that?"

"I wouldn't, but the cards say otherwise."

"Luckily, cards can't speak." I say.

"These ones do. They speak volumes. Would you like to know what they have to say about you?"

"No," I reply, gritting my teeth with uneasiness. A smile spreads across her face, perhaps agreeing to keep my secrets for me.

"What was the boy's name?" she asks.

"Luther," I state firmly.

"Yes ... He was the delivery boy. Came every week with the shipments that are stored in the attic."

"What kind of shipments?"

"Body shipments," she says harshly. Kyle and I exchange puzzled looks.

"Body shipments?" An idea came to mind, but there was no way in hell that could be it. Perhaps Luther wasn't as good of a boy as he had seemed. Maybe he had been evil all along. It's, in fact, usually always those ones that end up being the most sinister.

"He is conducting experiments ... on humans. He pays a great deal of money to get them shipped in and kept in their proper condition."

"John?" The idea of him killing a man seemed plausible, but experimentation?

"No." Beatrice shakes her head, dark curls falling over her face. "John simply transports the parts. The man you are seeking is named Clyde."

I search my brain, hoping I may have met him among my father's associates or politicians. This man was high up, for sure, to be able to afford the amount of money to get these items as well as paying off everyone at the docks and God knows who else in the city. Experimentation on humans? It made speakeasies look like child's play.

"Do you know where we can find him?"

She nods. "Yes. But you must be extremely careful. He's not a man to be trifled with."

"I understand. Thank you for your help."

She gives me an address and then returns to the deck in front of her. I feel Kyle's hand latch onto my waist, pulling me toward the door. It slips my mind too often that he's actually the enemy. A part of myself wishes he knew how foolish he was. If I was caught in that dilemma, wouldn't I want to know? I suppose I wouldn't. Oftentimes, it's better to know nothing than anything at all.

"Playing the gentleman now, are you?" I say as Kyle holds the door open for me. I'm shocked he has any manners at all.

"I mistook you for a lady," he replies.

"Big mistake," I warn, as I uncrumple the address Beatrice gave me with Kyle peering over my shoulder.

"It's near Storyville?" He was referring to a district in New Orleans that was populated with whorehouses. Well, Storyville didn't really exist anymore. It was deemed illegal several years ago and, since then, very few brothels were still in existence.

"Maybe Clyde prefers whores over ladies," I suggest. "Most men do."

"I don't," Kyle says sharply. "I prefer a woman who actually desires me."

I'm sure he thought I'd be so taken with him aching for genuine affection. I merely snickered at him. "Well then, I'm sure you've never been with a woman in that regard."

"And I'm sure you've been with many men," he shoots back coldly.

"I've been with enough."

"You think you can get in?" His voice seems to revert back to his usual matter-of-fact tone.

"To Clyde's?"

"Yes."

"Getting in is the easy part. Staying in will be tricky. Clyde, whoever he is, is smart. He'll most likely be able to smell an imposter from a mile away. Lucky for you, I've got experience."

VIII

KYLE and I arrive at the address Beatrice gave us. It's a large, dark blue house with white shutters. Its antebellum architecture mirrors the same structure of almost all the homes in the city. White pillars at the entrance, two sturdy columns surrounding the doorway, and nostalgia reeking from every inch of the premises. The balcony above was decadent and the home itself screamed old wealth and prestige, which was strange considering the circumstances which it was now in. From the outside, you would never guess a man so vile inhabited it.

The wind blew heavy, making the weeping willows around us bend and sway. The late afternoon sky dawned down on Kyle in repulsion, as though it refused to acknowledge his existence, but mostly those dark eyes which were eerily close to the image of sinkholes. I wanted to dig my fingers in his flesh, perhaps just to see if there was any warmth within him.

"I'm going in. Go home. I'll telephone you later when I'm inside."

"Are you afraid?" he asks. "Even just a little bit?"

"No," I reply. The truth is almost nothing frightens me anymore. Except him, I suppose. "I'm comforted by chaos, perhaps because it's all I've ever known."

His neck winds in toward me. He steps forward and I can feel my heart racing. I raise my chin up, curiously wondering if he will proceed to kiss me. He does not. Instead, he slips a switchblade into my coat pocket and whispers, "Give 'em hell."

I leave him at the bottom of the staircase and make my way up the steps to an arched door made of smooth wood. I look down at myself and begin rearranging my garments. I hike my emerald dress high up enough to reveal the place between my bare thighs and unbutton a few of my velvet buttons, revealing some cleavage. If I'm going to play the whore, I need to look the part.

I knock twice, hearing footsteps behind the door and shuffling; then, a few moments later, a girl who looks barely older than me stands before me. She's lovely, a brunette with curls down to her rib cage and heart-shaped lips. Her bright blue eyes were startling and I stood for a moment, admiring her.

"Hey baby," she purrs at me.

"Hello. I'm Audrey." I match the tone of her voice as I give her a sultry grin.

"I'm Rose," she replies. I wait at the door for a moment longer, peering in to get a small glimpse of the interior.

"Well, come on in, honey. I won't bite."

I step inside and immediately am taken aback by my surroundings. The house is very elegant. Much more alluring than most whorehouses I've been to, which look like abandoned mansions with rats for decor. No, this one was elegant. Satin love seats, velvet drapes, royal blues and purples on every surface. It was fit for royalty. And the girls looked like those straight out of the pictures.

Rose led me toward the dining room, where a few men were seated around a table, playing poker. The first man was hideous—he looked like a French bulldog. He was practically drooling on the beauty that sat on his lap. She was clearly trying to mask her contempt but not doing it too well. The man didn't seem to mind though, as he groped her breast with his right hand.

The other two men were rather decent-looking. I'm not sure if it was because they were seated next to a pig or because they were actually attractive. One man was focused on his cards. I could see his mind working, calculating, fixed on the task at hand. The third man sat looking rather content, smoking a cigarette and blowing the smoke into the mouth of a petite doll-like redhead with ravishing green eyes. She seemed amused with him as she opened and closed her mouth like a mouse playing chase with a cat. Rose showed me to the room as she began making introductions.

"Everyone, meet Audrey!" She giggles as she points toward the beauty on the pig's lap. "This is Adrianna. That's Hubert." Next, she points at the man deep in focus. "That's Jasper. He's an accountant—loves his numbers!" She goes on to the man smoking. "This is Clyde and that is Ivy." Ivy wiggles her fingers into a wave. I return her greeting with a grin. So this was Clyde. I study him subtly. He's handsome with light brown hair, brown eyes, and a charming smile. I pictured him in a lab coat with a scalpel in hand, standing over a dismembered torso. It didn't sit right in my mind, but then again looks are deceptive. I mean, I murdered someone and I don't appear to be monstrous either.

"Aren't you a sight for sore eyes?" Clyde reaches his hand out to shake mine. Said by any other man, those words would have sounded annoying, but from him they sounded like a compliment.

"You aren't so bad yourself," I respond. He gently nudges Ivy off his lap and whispers something in her ear. It was clearly devious, because she giggles and rushes up the staircase.

"So" — Clyde clears his throat — "what brings you to my house?" He exhales smoke out of his nose.

"I'm looking for work. A friend of mine recommended your house."

"Did she? Well ... I'm not particularly looking for new women, but you are quite a doll." I raise my chin and pout my lips.

"It's true."

"Assertive too. You must be deadly."

"You've got no idea."

He chuckles.

"Rose, show our new Audrey upstairs. Make her comfortable."

Rose grasps my arm and leads me up the grand staircase. It winds in the most beautiful fashion, as though it's leading us up toward the heavens. Rose's baby blue slip is a few sizes too small for her, but it compliments her curves. I assume that's why she chose it.

At the top of the staircase is a hallway that seems to stretch on for an eternity and that has far too many doors. A large oval window stands at the end of the hallway, letting light flood through, reflecting rays of sun off the glass door handles.

Rose opens a dark purple door on the right-hand side of the hallway. Inside is a queen-size bed with green silk sheets and a duvet. Above it is a beautiful white canopy that sways from a gust of wind outside. Two Victorian dressers stand adjacent to the bed and on the nightstand is a tower of candles glued together with wax. The bathroom has a French bathtub with gold-lined finishes on the rim. It also includes a vanity with a full-size mirror. To say it was decadent would be a vast understatement.

"How do you like it?" she asks, her doll eyes fluttering.

"It's certainly extravagant," I mutter as my eyes continue to explore the room, finding new details.

"Yes, you'll soon come to see everything here is. Clyde only provides us with the best. I can attest to that." She seems as though she'd been here so long the outside world had drifted from her conscience. Though I would hardly blame her for wanting to escape. One could only live in a dollhouse so long before becoming a doll oneself.

"Alright, well, I'll leave you to get settled before the men arrive. They usually arrive around eleven. They're generous with their attention and even more generous with their money, so you'll want to make the best impression you can."

With that, she scurried out of the room, her figure seeming to disappear into the walls. The door shut behind her with a thud, leaving me alone with my thoughts. I flung myself onto the bed, wondering if Kyle had made it home yet. Strangely, I missed his presence, even if I do despise him. In fact, I don't think I've ever despised a man more—except for my father, of course. Perhaps I'm secretly in love with Kyle. I've never been in love, but I've heard of it. Jack used to tell me stories of women he'd loved who tore his heart to pieces. Some of the jazz musicians at Vex play songs of lovers they had lost due to marriage and war.

It's often said that love consumes us completely. It eats us up and spits us all out just the same. I would never allow myself to share the same fate. I notice the sun beginning to set, letting the moon rise and drown us with her mischief. I close my eyes, allowing my body to sink into the soft sheets and forcing my racing thoughts to fade into oblivion.

IX

I'm awoken a few hours later to Rose shaking me profusely. "Wake up, sleepy head! You've gotta get dressed." I grunt as I roll out of bed onto the floor. I'd managed to take off my dress while I was sleeping and was now left only in my stockings and undergarments. I hear Rose rummaging through the closet, presumably to find something that will entice the suitors I'll meet tonight. I suppose, to keep up appearances, I'll have to let one of the men take me to bed. I'm no virgin. I've slept with many men, more than I can count, but always on my own accord.

"Rose," I call to her, my voice sluggish. I slowly lift my body to standing. She appears in front of me with an almost sheer beige slip.

"This will go superbly with your pearls and just a bit of rouge on your lips, wouldn't you agree?"

I wouldn't agree, but I had no time to argue.

"Where's the telephone?"

"In the bathroom, next to the vanity."

I give her an approving smile as I snatch the slip and slam the bathroom door behind me. I throw it on the vanity and run the bath, hoping to muffle out any sounds as I ring Kyle. I wait for a few moments, anxiously waiting to hear his voice.

"Hello." I feel myself able to breathe again. "Kyle."

"Alice, how the hell are you?" I would smack him if I could.

"I'm in. I met him," I whisper, "Clyde."

"Did you? What's he like?" I can hear the anticipation turning in his voice.

"He's not what I expected, that's for sure."

"Have you made any money yet?" I can feel him sneering over the phone.

"I don't have time for your moronic questions. I'm in a bind."

"Why? What kind of trouble?" His tone is suddenly serious.

"Just come by as soon as you can. Oh, and wear something tasteful. You're gonna spend a lot of money tonight." I hang up before he can respond. I reach for the slip on the vanity while inspecting myself in the mirror. I'm naturally thin, leaving my ribs and hip bones visible. I always loved how boney I am, a skeleton with a thin layer of flesh keeping me somewhere between life and death. My thighs never meet and my chest is small as can be.

I must have gotten my genetics from my father's side because my mother was voluminous. I remember watching her paint on the balcony in the mornings in nothing but her undergarments. I pull the slip over my head and down my body. It's flattering to my thin frame but quite exposing. I've worn provocative garments before but nothing quite as revealing as this. I noticed an assortment of makeup and perfume on a silver tray on the bathroom counter. I help myself to it, spraying what smells like rose water on my neck and applying some rouge to my lips and powder to compliment my soft complexion.

I stand there for a while, admiring this lovely bathroom in this luxurious whorehouse and almost losing sight of who I was or why I was here. It's easy to get lost when no one cares to find you, I suppose. I could stay here for days without my father even wondering about my whereabouts. I take one last glance in the mirror before heading downstairs.

I reach the bottom of the staircase to find men swarming the house, smoking cigarettes while whores try their best to seduce them. I glimpse Rose on a tall, lanky man's arm. Her head tips back as she laughs hysterically. Her voice rings through the dining room and people begin to take notice, turning their heads and muttering things under their breath. She seems blissfully unaware of herself as the fellow she's with continues whispering amusing things to her.

I don't realize that I've been standing still at the foot of the staircase until I feel a hand on my waist. A smile creeps over my lips as I turn around, expecting to see Kyle at my side. Instead, it's Clyde. Startled, I pull away slightly. I can smell the gin on his breath. It's the sweetest scent in the world. His tie is undone, falling down his dressing shirt. I put my hands on his chest and began fixing his tie.

"Thank you, baby," he says to me. In response, I snatch the glass from his hand and drain every drop. He laughs, showing all his teeth. "Would you care for another drink?"

I could take a bottle at this point. "Yes. Bourbon, please."

He pours me a drink from a nearby table. I keep my eyes glued to the door, waiting for Kyle to enter through it at any moment. An hour passes and I find myself hiding on a love seat near the kitchen. A few suitors had already come up to me, interested in taking me upstairs, but I had given them the cold shoulder. As the night drifted on, I knew my time was running out. Clyde would not accept me here if I didn't sleep with a man and earn my keep. So I kept drinking, hoping to drown out the voices around me but even more so the one in my head. It takes much more alcohol these days to soothe myself.

I watch out the window at the moon in her crescent form while clouds drift beneath and sometimes cover her completely, but only for a little while before she reappears once more, illuminating the night sky.

"Alice." I feel a tap on my shoulder. My eyes meet his. His dark, never-ending eyes that make me feel as though I'm being hypnotized.

"Kyle." I breathe his name as though it's the last word I'll ever speak. He looks around, agitated.

"Where is he? Where is the son of a bitch?"

"Calm yourself," I scold him. "Now is not the time to lose your composure."

"Fine, fine." He fidgets with his pockets as he lights up a cigarette. He exhales, his eyes scanning the room like a hunter trying to secure his prey.

"You look handsome," I compliment him in the most insulting way possible. His eyes are suddenly fixed on mine. It's true, he does look dashing in his black dinner jacket, waistcoat, and slacks. "I almost mistook you for an adequate suitor."

He laughs. "Don't. I'm not here to save you."

I laugh, but only because his presence proves otherwise.

"I'd be concerned if you were." I snatch the cigarette from his hand, proceeding to take a lengthy drag, exhaling and enveloping us both in smoke.

"Seen any men you would take to bed?"

He doesn't seem to fit in at all with the other men. Even dressed appropriately, he couldn't seem to be further from them.

"Not one in sight." They would bore me, surely.

"Not even me?"

"Especially not you," I taunt, unable to keep myself from grinning.

"Ahhh!—" Screeching and the shattering of glass echo from across the room. "Get off me! You pig!"

It's Rose screaming at Hubert. Her dress is pulled down, revealing her right breast and a trickle of blood running down her slip. Hubert cowers in the corner with his eyes lowered to the ground. Rose runs at him, pounding her hand against his head and crying hysterically. I see Clyde storm into the room and pull her off him.

"Let's go upstairs," I say to Kyle. He nods and in the middle of the commotion we slip upstairs to my bedroom. As I slam the door shut behind me, I see him standing at the window, his figure reminding me of a shadow—tall, thin, and dark. He pulls back the drapes and stares out into the night.

"It's certainly an elegant brothel," he says.

"Yes, not quite like any I've seen before," I reply. Clyde certainly had a taste for elegance. I wouldn't be surprised if he came from old money.

"I'm surprised you've stayed this long. I assumed you would never go this far to uncover Luther's murderer." My eyes wander everywhere else in the room, not daring to meet his.

"You shouldn't underestimate me," I say daringly as I sit on the edge of the luxurious bed, my head leaning against the old wooden frame, my hands folded over one another on my lap.

"Yes, you proved me quite wrong." His lips curl as though they are going to form a grin—only for a moment though.

"It's easy to prove others wrong when they seem to expect nothing from you." I should know, my father expected nothing but the worst from me. Though, in his defense, I usually proved him right in that regard.

"That's true. I'm often never expected to be true to my word, especially from those I owe it to most." His eyes gaze off, as though he's remembering a time when others had faith in him.

"Is that so?"

"Unfortunately. I promised my brother we would be alright, that eventually the pain would ease and the days wouldn't drag on as they seemed to."

"After your parents passed?"

"Yes, and now he's rotting in the ground, after a mere year no less. He was only fifteen and even though I'm only two years older, I'm still his older brother. I was supposed to take care of him. Some kind of brother I am." His expression darkens. The disgust he had for himself reeked. Anyone with eyes could see it.

"An awfully good one," I muse, mocking him slightly.

"You could never comprehend what it's like to be alone, truly alone. I have no one, and when I die, the world will go on and it will have meant nothing to anyone," he spits. Coming from anyone else, those words would have sounded like a cry for help, but from him they only seemed true.

"You shouldn't be so rough on yourself," I say as I reach out, my hand grasping his firmly.

"Why not? Wouldn't you if you lost a brother?" It was almost a whisper, his anger seeming to form clouds around his sadness.

"No," I say coldly.

He leans in toward me, his dark, boney figure towering above me, sending shivers down my spine.

"Well, you don't have one. Maybe that's why."

Our eyes meet intensely. He looks soulless.

"Maybe."

His darkness was so enticing, I was unable to break away from him. Our lips were mere inches apart, daring to meet. I waited for him to pursue me, but he did not. He merely laid down next to me, consumed by his thoughts. The rest of the night was spent in silence, lying next to one another, the party raging on underneath us, the sounds of awful laughter and beautiful melodies of jazz weaving together.

At that moment, there was no Luther, no father to scold me, no city crawling with lunatics just beyond the door. There was only us. Kyle held me captive in his arms as the sun rose, replacing the moon for the day to begin. Hours passed by as we lay with one another, bracing ourselves for the dark days ahead that were sure to come.

X

It's cold when I awaken. The bed is empty and Kyle has vanished sometime during the evening. I loathe how much I wish I could have woken up still in his arms, our bodies tangled together, safe from the world surrounding us. Neither of us had actually admitted to caring for one another, no matter how apparent it seemed. We maintained an attraction that I did not fully understand and, even though I knew whatever we had could not be, part of me was ignorant to it. Deep down, I was foolish enough to hold onto the hope that he would never find out what I'd done.

Maybe part of me wants him—wants him to be the one to fix the world I was in, which I deemed to be the root of all my troubles. I love his company even when I despise him. I find myself craving his attention in every form. I yearn for our passionate moments and, even more, for our arguments. It felt as though I'd met my match.

Sighing, I brush those thoughts away. I needed to focus on the task at hand. I was here to frame Clyde, make him into a murderer. I was here to make Clyde Luther's murderer. I put on a silk robe I found in the closet and made my way downstairs. The house was deserted in the morning hours and seemed much larger than it had during the evening. I assumed all the occupants were still resting after a long night spent pleasing men.

I searched through every drawer and shelf I could find, but managed to find nothing that I imagined I would. I envisioned boxes of human parts organized neatly and labeled, hidden in his closet, and an assortment of medical instruments in the bathroom drawers. A madman physician who believed he was a god, believed he could overpower God. Yes, that would be a marvelous ending for Luther. Kyle would be even more enraged, thinking of all the ways in which his brother's body had been dismembered and used. All the rage he had stored for me would be released onto Clyde, and once all was said and done, he would be free of it.

I had to calm the excitement that began to rise within me, thinking of how relieved I would be once this was all over. I still wondered what Clyde was even looking for in his experiments with his passion which seemed too great to bear. I needed to find evidence to give to Kyle, and soon, before I would surely have to take my next suitor. Clyde must leave the house sometime, I supposed. I'd have to wait him out.

XI

I SPENT the afternoon drinking heavily and playing cards with Adrianna and Ivy. I enjoyed their company and for a little while was able to forget about the outside world. Adrianna was nineteen and Ivy eighteen, and it had felt like the first time I'd ever spent time with girls my own age before. Especially in a setting outside of a smoke-filled, foul speakeasy.

At this moment, we were merely teenage girls acting as we were meant to. We smoked and played and I won the first two rounds. That was, until Ivy proposed we make a rule that the losers must down a glass of bourbon for every loss. Then I purposely lost the next two rounds.

We laughed as we played, joking about the events from the previous night and Rose's tantrum. I listened to their stories, intrigued by their courage. Adrianna explained that she was brought up in a wealthy family in Baton

Rouge and was supposed to wed a man who ran an oil trade. She went on about how terrible this man was, how he groped her the first night he met her at a dinner party on her family's estate. How she tried to tell her mother that he was not for her and begged them to reconsider.

She tells me she made it to her wedding day and as she approached the aisle and almost said her vows, she fled—in her wedding gown, no less. She took a train to New Orleans and never looked back. She admits to wanting to telephone or write her family, but she was worried that they'd come after her and try to drag her back to that wretched man.

"If I wouldn't have met Clyde, I don't know where I'd be," she explains.

"Married to a pig? Living in a mansion?" Ivy suggests. Adrianna rolls her eyes at her.

"So, you want to stay here? Forever?" I ask.

"Well, honey, I'm not going to be beautiful forever. I'll need to find myself a man sometime." She lights up a cigarette as she throws down her next card. "But in the meantime, I get to live here and do as I please. It's a better bargain than what I would get back home. That's for damn sure."

I don't ask her any more questions. I could understand why she would want to run away. Maybe all young girls were rebellious and adventurous, some just more honest about it than others.

"So, Audrey, where are you from?"

"Here. New Orleans." If I'd learned anything about lying, it was to keep the conversations as short as possible. Lying about where you're from is an amateur mistake I'd made before and it had landed me in more than a few brawls.

"What brought you to our house?" Rose pipes in over my shoulder, her high-pitched voice straining my ears.

"My parents died in an automobile accident a few months ago and I have no other family. None that I know of, anyways."

I could feel their sympathetic eyes on me. I let my eyes fall to the ground and managed to get a single tear to fall down my cheek. Rose swings both her arms around me and holds me so tight I can hardly breathe.

"Aww, Audrey! You're home now, baby!"

I grimace, waiting for it to be over.

"You know, a girl as pretty as you could find a nice man." It came from Ivy who sat on the chair across from me, looking composed.

"I would, but you see, I like to do what I want, when I want, with whomever I want." I grab a cigarette from the case on the table and light it with a match.

"That kind of attitude will get you nowhere, honey," Ivy says.

I already knew this. I would never be the type of woman to marry or bear children. I was a lone wolf, a fictional character. I wasn't made to last forever.

"Don't listen to her. Don't let her worry you." Adrianna places her hand on my lower arm.

"I never do," I respond, while I exhale smoke from my nostrils.

"Well, I agree with her!" Rose said. Of course she does. I doubt any man will ever be able to hold her down. She's got far too much fire in her.

"Rose, you'll agree with anything just for the sake of arguing," Ivy says coldly.

"I do not!" she squeals like a child.

"Please. Remember that day when the sheriff came by and you tried to hassle him and one of his men. What was his name?"

"Edward!" Adrianna says. Ivy laughs wickedly.

"Yes! Ed! And Rose was going on and on about how he should take her to the pictures and then the sheriff butts in and says" — she leans in close as she mimics his voice — "know your place, young lady." Rose's face turns beet red and she begins shaking as though she's about to go into a frenzy.

"Girls, girls." Clyde comes down the staircase and pulls Rose into his arms. "Get along now. I won't have you turning this into a madhouse."

Rose cuddles into his chest, rubbing her hair up against him. Ivy rolls her eyes as she turns to me and mouths, "Crybaby." I merely grin at her in response.

In moments like these, I'm almost relieved that I live alone with my father. I imagine this is what it would be like to have siblings. Constant dramatics and malicious remarks that come to no end. When I was younger, I always wished I had a sibling. Someone to keep me company, someone to play hide-and-seek with. Someone to sleep with when my father would be away all night on "business," leaving me alone in the house, hiding under the covers while listening to the wind screech outside my windows.

That was near the time I found refuge in the moon and her lovingness. Even as a child, I knew I could never put my trust in humanity. Humans lie, steal, and covet their desires above everything else. I, myself, am not exempt from these traits. And at only fifteen, I cannot imagine what will become of me in the years to come. It only gets worse from here. I excuse myself from the girls, claiming I must make a telephone call. I flee to my room and lock myself safely in the bathroom. I decide to ring my father.

"Hello." His deep, manly voice echoes in my ear.

"Father ... it's me ... Alice." I wait for him to begin yelling at me. To ask me where I've been for the past two days, threaten me with what will happen if I don't return immediately.

"Alice, why are you calling? I'm about to go into a business meeting."

“Aren’t you upset with me?” My voice is shaky. I already know he has no idea that I’ve gone, but I ask him anyway, letting the child in me remain hopeful.

“For what? Are you in trouble again, Alice?”

He sighs. I can feel his displeasure over the phone.

“No. I’m fine.” I slam the telephone down with all my might.

My body heats up with a mixture of anger and sadness. I can’t tell where one begins and the other ends. I feel tears welling up in my eyes, but I don’t dare let them roll down my cheeks. I wouldn’t waste tears over my father. I hear the front door shut loudly and I walk over to the window near the tub. I pull back the curtains and see Clyde rushing down the street. About time. This was my shot. I didn’t know how long he was going to be gone for or the next time he was going to leave the house. I had to make the most of this opportunity.

I tiptoe out of my room and down the hall, examining each door on the second floor. They all seemed to share the same height and width, except one. At the far end of the hallway, furthest away from the staircase, one door was larger than the rest. I glide down the hall, my stockings brushing up against the wood floor, leaving me silent as a mouse. I reach my hand out to turn the knob and the door opens with a click. I exhale in relief that it was not locked.

I wonder how someone hiding so much could be so careless. Either way, it works to my advantage. I open the door slowly, letting the contents of the room fill my sight. His room was not the horror-filled chamber I had envisioned. In fact, it was rather simple. His room was large with a king-size bed and a dresser but not much else. I slide my hands across the bed and notice that the sheets are made of cotton and not silk like my room. There was a rug which desperately needed to be dusted and his closet held only a few garments.

There was a dark wooden desk near the window that had a few photographs and papers laid out. I studied the photographs more closely. One was of him and Rose seated on the sofa in the living room. Another was of him and another man dressed nicely in their pin-striped suits. The last one, though, caught my eye. No, it couldn't be. Was it my father? I looked closely at it and, sure enough, it was Clyde and my father. They stood next to one another holding glasses of what I presume was bourbon, smiling as though they had just completed a mutually successful business deal. I turned the photo over and, on the back, written in ink, was inscribed, "Clyde and Benjamin W., 1907."

A million ideas ran through my mind. First of all, it could mean nothing. I mean, my father was a prominent businessman and extremely well-known throughout the city. They could have met in a number of ways. But something told me there was more. I needed to find out if my suspicions were true. I would have to get Clyde alone to find out what he knew.

I slipped out of his room as undetectably as I had come in. I could hear the girls shuffling through clothing and fixing their makeup for the night's event. I wandered down to the kitchen, looking for my next drink. I couldn't remember the last time I'd eaten and, quite frankly, didn't care. Booze and cigarettes are enough to sustain me these days.

I find a bottle of bourbon in the kitchen cabinet and curl up near the window. I nursed the bottle in my lap and let my head hit up against the glass window. I watched as two lovers kissed passionately outside underneath the streetlamp. They looked only a few years older than I, but their passion seemed timeless. The boy had his fingers entwined in her soft, dark curls while her arms were swung around his neck, pressing his lips to hers. They looked so far away. I'm sure their minds were lost in each other's bodies, their senses nourished with the utmost pleasure. I wondered where they came from. What was her father like? Where did they meet? How long did they have before their fates were decided and they could not be? I imagined them years from now, having moved on from one another, living separate lives, promised to other people.

That's just how it is in the world. Nothing good ever lasts. I suppose it's good that it does not. If it did, we would eventually be unsatisfied, nauseated, bored. Humans need to be taken away from the things we love most or we'll forget why we ever loved them so much.

I spent most of the night huddled up in the kitchen, drinking myself further and further into oblivion. By the time I finished the last drop of the bottle, the moon was well into her form. My vision was blurred and my body numb. I watched myself rise from the nook and stumble my way into the living room. It was swarming with men, the scent of cigarettes, and the whores in their finest garments. I had to cling to the wall so I didn't completely lose my footing. I see Clyde standing on the opposite side of the room and manage to get to him without causing a scene. He turns when I'm within inches from him. I'm sure he can smell the stench of alcohol on my tongue. The men he was talking to exchange looks with one another, obviously not taken with my state. I ignore them and focus any attention I have left on Clyde.

"You are one baby vamp." It didn't come from Clyde but one of the men seated behind him.

"Watch your mouth," I spit back at him.

"Come on, doll, you're indisposed. I'll put you to bed." It came from Clyde. As he wove his arm around my waist and ushered me up the staircase, I felt like I was floating. I could hear our footsteps but couldn't feel a thing.

Clyde led me to my room where he placed me gently on the bed. He fluffed a pillow and placed it behind my head before covering the silk sheets over my small frame. I looked up at him, wondering how someone so evil could also be so gracious.

"How did someone so young end up here?" he asks with concerned eyes. I should have felt insulted by his question, but instead I simply wondered how I had come to be this way at such a young age.

"I don't know, sometimes they choose you."

"Who does?"

"Dreadful people, vile habits, unlucky timing."

"You think God is plotting against you?"

"I don't believe in God. If he does exist, it would seem as though he's plotting against all of us."

"You shouldn't spend so much time sulking. It won't improve your condition."

"And what do you suggest I do? Try to fix a smile while the world is burning?"

"The world never burns for long. The rain comes eventually."

"I'm sick of waiting for it then."

"It's always difficult when you're young. There is much you can't comprehend now."

"Maybe I don't want to comprehend. Maybe I just want it to stop."

"It will stop. You will grow, your dreams will grow, and you will change."

"Did you ever have dreams?"

"I had dreams greater than God himself."

"That seems far too large. One would think dreams which stretch to the end of the city would suffice."

"No, not mine. I was going to be a great physician. I was at the top of my class in university. I had never loved anything more." He smiled as he spoke, his eyes gleaming wildly.

"Why did you end up not pursuing it?"

He sighs. "There was an incident in the lab ... I'd prefer not to discuss it. Besides, it's late and you need your rest."

"Yes, I could use some."

I drift off, closing my eyes and letting my nightmares take me once again.

XII

THE next day, I'm in the bathtub smoking a cigarette. The sound of water filling a tub reminds me of my mother, when I would sit on her vanity watching her bathe. She looked like a Roman goddess, effortlessly ravishing. I barely even knew her, yet I miss her. I didn't even know it was possible to yearn for someone so much who you hardly knew anything about.

I remember, once, I told Jack about how I felt. I was around eleven, weeping at the bar silently while telling him how I wished for her. Jack told me that those who yearn for the unknown are romantics. I have been telling Jack all of my secrets for as long as I can remember. Even though Jack's loyalty was to my father, he was like an uncle to me and he'd kept many secrets for me in the past. He kept supplying me booze, even though he knew my father disapproved of my habit, and didn't tell my father of the many gentlemen I went home with.

My father found out most things, of course. People always fed him information on me, hoping it would put them on his good side. It had worked in the beginning when I first began to rebel, but now had become so frequent my father didn't bat an eyelash at the horrendous stories he was informed of on a regular basis.

I cover my hair with soap, washing through my golden blonde bob. When I was a child, my hair reached my hips, but by the time I was twelve I took a pair of scissors to the bathroom and locked myself in. I decided hair was a drag and I was better off without it. My father, displeased as usual, yelled at me for it for an hour.

I continue to wash myself, my petite figure barely taking up space in the large tub. I open the window, letting the fresh air whirl the steam from the hot water around. It seemed hard to grasp that Clyde could truly be a mad scientist. He possessed such a calm and handsome demeanor, it was difficult to imagine him in a lab coat with blood all over his hands. But I suppose the most deranged men were often very well-kept. I mean, how else could they manage to not get caught?

Too frenzied with all my thoughts, I decide I needed to call Kyle immediately to get a second opinion. I hop out of the tub, my feet slipping on the marble floor as I reach for a towel, wrapping it around my body like a mummy. I sit down at the vanity, water dripping down my hair onto the velvet seat. I pick up the telephone and wait for Kyle's voice on the opposite end.

"Hello." Hearing his voice made me miss him. I love how certain his voice always is.

"I have news," I say in my childlike tone.

"Alice." He sounds relieved, almost delighted to hear that it's me.

"You'll never guess what our man went to university to be?" I run my fingers through my hair, combing out the knots with my left hand.

"What?"

I expected a playful answer, but he didn't seem to be in the mood.

"A physician."

"Well, well. Looks like Beatrice was telling the truth."

"It seems so. I knew I liked something about her," I say.

"So, should I come now and put a bullet in his head and we can be on our way?" he says.

"Don't be foolish. We don't even know if he was the one who killed Luther. He could just be a piece of the puzzle."

It would have been a perfect opportunity to pin Luther's death on Clyde, but seeing that photo of him and my father intrigued me. I needed to know what the connection was.

"Anyway, I'm leaving today," I say. "I think I'm finished here."

"I'll come meet you," he says firmly.

"No ... I have some things I have to take care of. I'll see you soon."

With that, I hang up and begin getting dressed. I was aching to see him and wasn't sure why I was denying him so.

I swing open my bedroom door and walk down the grand staircase to the living room—not a soul in sight, perfect. I could slip out without notice. As I carefully open the front door I hear a voice behind me: "Where are you going?"

It was Ivy. Damn. I swing around to see her standing in a black silk robe tied around her waist. Her red hair was unbrushed and wild, and she held a cigarette in her right hand, eyes narrowed at me. I keep my cool, hoping to keep this encounter as short as possible.

"I have some errands to attend to," I say. Her eyes search me suspiciously.

"What kind of errands?"

God, was she always like this?

"I have to pick up a dress from the tailors."

She raises her eyebrows.

"You know, we have people who do that for us." Agitated, I tap my foot on the floor.

"Look, Ivy, I'm in a rush. I'll explain when I return." I wouldn't, of course, because I wouldn't be coming back. She opened her mouth as though she was going to say something, but I turned before she could, dashing out the door, leaving nothing but the sound of the wind.

XIII

THAT night, I was heading to Vex. It was half past midnight and the night was alive as ever. Howling laughter filled the streets from pedestrians with the stench of alcohol on their breath.

I arrive at the entrance. The doorman, Walter, stands keeping watch as usual. Walter has a large, muscular figure, rough skin akin to leather, and more scars than I'd ever seen on a man. I'd seen Walter take down many men, most of which was entertaining, but sometimes bordered on partially demented, which was unsurprising. If anything, he was on the lesser side of evil that I'd encountered—much less. If I'd learned anything, true evil was located in a man's mind, not his body. I would be frightened if I hadn't known him for so long.

My father had found him on the street. He'd been fighting for money to get by, but seemed to tire of the lifestyle. My father had seen potential in him and dragged him into this world, where he has remained since. My father seemed to have a habit of finding lost souls and turning them into horrid creatures like himself.

When he saw me approach, Walter's expression turned vacant. Saying he disliked me was an understatement. He'd made it pretty clear that he disapproved of me even being allowed in Vex.

I try to push past him, but he puts his arm in front of me. "Passcode?"

I scowl at his question. "Walter, move," I say glaring at him.

"Does your father know you're coming in tonight?"

"What is this? An interrogation? I'm not in the mood."

My flask was once again empty and I was parched. The scent of alcohol in the air was only worsening my cravings.

"Fine."

He moved to the side and let me through. I stormed inside, going straight to the bar. I sat at my usual spot at the very end—the best seat in the house, as I always say. I enjoy it because I can see everyone but they cannot see me. It was dark with only a candle in front of me, illuminating my eyes like a cat. I prop my elbows up on the counter as Jack sets a glass in front of me filled with gin.

I dislike Vex yet spend so much of my time here it feels like a second home. It's sad how much time I spend here. I'm only a child yet I wander around a speakeasy as if it's a playground.

I remember when my father opened it in 1920, when it was just an old, abandoned bank. Most of his men were opposed to the space, thinking it would take far too long and cost too much to remodel. My father would not budge, he had made his decision and he was too stubborn in his ways. He predicted Vex would be the most renowned speakeasy in New Orleans, with the purest alcohol and most talented musicians. Within a year, all of this came true. Every well-known flapper, socialite, and business tycoon had made Vex their usual spot.

"Alice." Jack's voice brought me out of my thoughts. I look up to see him leaning on the bar. He's wearing a black button-down shirt and dark trousers. He looks out of breath, which is expected considering how full the bar is tonight. "Where've you been lately? Haven't seen you around much."

I'd been caught up trying to fix all the chaos I'd caused from that one night. The night I'd murdered Luther, which still remained a mystery as to why I'd done it. I couldn't recall any feeling at all, simply images of myself butchering him, images which the demons in my nightmares now seemed to taunt me with.

"You know, same old, same old," was all I replied. I did not want to speak of Luther. Listening to Kyle go on about his brother was enough agony for me.

"Getting into trouble? Drinking?" Jack suggested.

"It would be troubling if I was acting any other way."

"Yes, I'd be quite concerned about you."

"Jack?"

"Yes?"

"What if you met someone who understood you completely? Someone who you had always hoped to meet or dreamt of, but never actually thought they could exist."

"Well, I'd do anything I could to keep them."

"What if you didn't know if they would love you the way you would love them?"

"In matters of the heart, you will never know for sure whether someone will be true to you and, almost always, you can expect disappointment."

"Disappointment seems to be the only constant." My eyes cast downward.

"Do you think you're in love, Alice?"

"Would I be too foolish if I was?"

"No, but you must be careful. It can be dangerous."

"I'm sure I've endured worse."

"Falling in love is about the most dangerous thing there is. Trust me, I've seen about all there is out there. We lose our sanity. We become crazed zombies. The way you chase booze is the same way love gets you. It gets its hold on you and you'll do anything for it."

"I think I lost all reason long ago, Jack. It seems I don't have anything to lose anymore."

The truth is, I can't recall a time when I had any reason at all. Even before Kyle, I had been a lost cause. Maybe Kyle was just the point of no return, the end to the nothing that was my life. My empty, hollow life that I have spent by filling it with sleepless nights, booze, and jazz records that seem to spin on endlessly.

"Well then, you must be the deadliest woman in the room."

XIV

PACING back and forth in my bedroom the following afternoon, I feel an overwhelming sense of urgency to take control of my life. The strangeness of the world around me only seemed to be increasing, leading my mind to places from which I desperately wanted to escape. I couldn't get the photograph of my father and Clyde out of my head. I longed for it to be nothing, but the truth is nothing is random, especially in New Orleans. Secrets seem to be embedded in the city itself, hiding behind every corridor and even inside the most average-looking person.

I can't say I would be shocked if my father was caught up in a scheme with Clyde. I know he is truly capable of anything, but even though we have our disagreements, he's family—my own flesh and blood and the only person I have, even if I wish he wasn't most of the time. I had to know the truth.

Something told me John would be the one that would provide me with the answers I was seeking. If I'd learned anything from my father, it was that bribery and bloodshed were the two most effective ways of deriving information, and since I did not currently have a stash of cash at my disposal, I decided bloodshed would have to suffice.

I rang Jack and convinced him to gather a few of my father's men under the radar for an excursion. I ruffled through my garments, deciding on a satin black drop-waist, dark stockings, and my beat up Mary Janes. If things got bloody, my appearance wouldn't be too ruined. I examine myself in the mirror as I apply a shade of deep red rouge to my pouty, heart-shaped lips. I felt like a gangster trapped in the body of a woman. Deadly and delicious. I reach for my bottle of gin laying at my feet and take a swing, leaving red stains on the rim from my lips. I hear an automobile arrive outside. It was time.

I dash down the stairs to find Jack waiting for me, looking cool, his hands placed casually in his pockets, a devilish grin placed on his lips as if preparing himself for whatever mischievous plans I have in store for him. He has brought along three men with him. Their faces are shadowed by cigar smoke. They seem to be slightly different versions of one another, standing tall and statuesque. The gloomy day and light rain that falls compliment the sleek, dark gray automobile they arrive in, creating just the right atmosphere for what I had in mind.

Jack opens the door for me and I slide inside, adjusting myself comfortably on the leather seats as I light up a cigarette.

"I appreciate you doing this for me" I say, exhaling.

I've never asked him for a favor such as this one, although I've also never been caught in a dilemma of this magnitude.

"No problem, Alice. But tell me, what is this about?"

I take another drag before responding. "It would take far too long to explain."

I look out the window, wondering if the regret I felt would ever wear off.

“Does this have something to do with what we were discussing last night? Have you fallen in love?”

I shift my body slightly, so I’m facing him directly. “I’m unsure, but certainly trying everything in my power not to.”

“Is he involved somehow with this man we are going to see?”

“He could not be further from involved with anyone.”

“Maybe that is why he is so enticing.”

“Maybe. But as you know already, people who possess that effect are not to be trusted.”

“That’s wise. Always stay ahead of your enemies.”

“Yes. As strange as it sounds, he has grown to become both my enemy and also closest ally.” As I said the words, I wondered why I hadn’t come to that conclusion sooner. It was blisteringly obvious.

“Where are we headed?” It came from one of the men in the front seat, who was clearly fed up with my chatter.

“The docks,” I say loud enough for the driver to hear. I lock eyes with him in the rearview mirror and he nods, confirming my request. A moment later, we speed off through the French Quarter and I hope that, soon enough, Kyle would be an enemy no longer. I’d had more than enough enemies and not nearly enough friends.

XV

The docks stink as it is, the rain only causing them to seem even more atrocious. I'm forced to drag my already beat-up Mary Janes through puddles as I lead Jack and the others to find John, dodging men with crates until reaching the door that I remember fondly, if only for the memory of pushing Kyle through it. I twist the knob and the door opens, revealing John who sits, barely noticeable, at the opposite end of the room.

His eyes shoot up and focus on mine.

"You again," he spits.

"Yeah, me," I smile wickedly.

"Hold him down," I demand of the man beside me.

John's eyes flicker with fear as he makes an attempt to flee, but he's not quick enough. He's large but is overpowered and forced back down into his chair.

"What do you want?" he says.

"What do I want?" I say, my eyes narrowing at him. "You've got some real nerve giving me attitude when I could have every bone in your body broken with just a word." I strut closer to him, dragging out my words with each step. "I want the truth. Give me anything less and I'll have these boys put a bullet in your brain. But not before they pick out every one of your teeth." John swallows hard and seems to soften his grip. It's a shame he's submitting so quickly, further proving even large men who appear courageous can cower like children.

"I didn't kill the kid."

"Your eyes seem to say otherwise." The eyes always seem to give everyone away. It's the one thing that cannot be hidden. He looks down, reluctant. I motion to the man on my right. He proceeds to break one of John's fingers, the cracking of bones almost causing me to flinch. John screeches, trying to endure the pain.

"Why does he matter so much to you?" he says breathlessly.

"He doesn't. I'm curious as to how you had already been informed of his death before Kyle and I had even arrived that day."

"You stupid little girl ... you have no idea how far all this goes." He begins laughing uncontrollably. "I bet you couldn't wrap your little brain around it if you tried."

"Try me," I say, challenging him.

"Maybe I will tell you, just to take pleasure in watching you go get yourself killed." Part of me wanted to be afraid, but I wouldn't let myself. I had survived this long without letting fear consume me. I wasn't going to give in now.

"His name is Craven Lyles."

"Craven Lyles," I say. It didn't sound familiar.

"You don't know him," John says smugly.

"How do you know?" I say sharply. I was losing patience with him.

"If you did, you would be running by now."

"Who is he? And no more snide remarks. I'm done playing nice."

"He's a hitman who comes from the West. He's as cold-blooded as they come."

"He doesn't sound special."

"Sure, if you think having two different-colored eyes is ordinary."

"That proves nothing." Though it was interesting. It reminded me of a magic act I saw when I was a child. The magician was able to alter the color of his right eye using a trick of light. "Craven Lyles, huh? I guess I'll be seeing him real soon then."

Satisfied, I give my final request to Jack. "Beat him until he loses consciousness. Oh, and get an address too."

"Remember, it's your funeral!" John shrieks at me as I storm out of the room, leaving only the sounds of his screams behind me.

XVI

LATER that night, I'm sitting by the telephone in the dining room. I'm about to ring Kyle when I hear my father's footsteps. I always can tell him by his steps, because he practically stomps everywhere he goes. I expect him to keep walking up the stairs, ignoring my presence, but instead he proceeds to sit next to me. It's rare that we spend any time alone. If we're in the same room together, it's usually his office, where we remain constantly surrounded by the usual occupants of Vex: gangsters awaiting orders, flappers desperate for his attention, or musicians making noise to fill the void between us. But at the moment, there is nothing to distract us, no one to interrupt us. The house seems to become still, as though it too is waiting to see what awful argument we will engage in tonight.

"I'm in no mood to argue tonight," I say. My eyes remain fixed on the telephone, refusing to even look at him directly.

"I've come with no argument," my father replies. I don't believe him for a moment.

"What could you possibly have to say to me, then?" I feel the warmth of his hand as he places it over mine.

"I've only come to remind you that, as my only daughter, I will take care of you always."

"How commendable of you. A father who would take care of his daughter? Why, I've never heard of such a thing."

"You have every right to be upset with me. I haven't been the easiest of fathers to have."

"That we can both agree on."

"Do not whine, Alice. It does not become you."

"You did not teach me to be becoming. You've only shown me pain and violence."

"I taught you how to be strong, how to survive! You have no idea what the real world is like."

I turn my head sharply as I let the rage inside myself loose, spitting out feelings I've kept inside for far too long. "I have every idea thanks to you! The world did not corrupt me—you did. By ostracizing me from the world, not letting me go to school, by only teaching me how to survive in the world you created for me."

"You will grow into a powerful woman one day, Alice, and you will thank me for what I've done—for making you strong."

"Why? Because my mother was weak?" I say bitterly. She had chosen to end her life, something my father and I never discussed.

"Don't you dare speak of your mother that way!" His fist slams on the table, causing me to flinch. For a moment, we both breathe heavily. Remorse hangs thick in the air between us. There had been much said and yet piles upon piles of more things yet to be said. Straightening his tie, my father composes himself once more.

"Your mother was unfit to handle the cruelties of the world. What happened to her was a tragedy."

It truly had been. I couldn't begin to count how many times I've wished my mother would have lived through it. I wondered how much different I could have been with her input. My father knew nothing of how to raise a daughter. I was evidence of that.

"It was an awful tragedy." The words escape my mouth as merely a whisper.

Nothing else was said after that. Perhaps the pain that we both felt in that moment was too consuming to leave anything else to say; we sat for a while longer, listening to the wind before the phone rang and my father went out into the night to live up to his reputation as an infamous gangster.

XVII

I HAD rung Kyle and informed him about Craven Lyles, this supposedly exceptional hitman. As I had anticipated, his response was to impulsively murder whoever this mysterious man was, which is why I precisely asked that he not make any decisions without my approval. He agreed—reluctantly, of course.

I felt inclined to meet this man face to face and see what he knew. John's outright fear of him had piqued my curiosity. As I sat down at the bar at Vex that afternoon, I wondered what his involvement was in all this. Was he caught up with Clyde? Or perhaps my father? It seemed that no one was to be trusted these days. Often, I wish we would all stop keeping so many secrets. Everyone in town seemed to be harboring more than a few, and with all of us in such close proximity, I felt there was no room to breathe anymore.

I drum my fingers on the shiny dark wooden surface, a glass of gin laying in my opposite hand. I wore a cream, chiffon dress that reached down to my calves and had little velvet buttons that started at the top of my neck and trickled down my waistline. I shift positions and look around the club. Vex is stale as the afternoon light spills in through the stained glass windows above the bar. The love seats are dusty and stained and the musicians look worn out from practicing their repetitive tunes over and over. I hear my father from all the way up in his office barking orders through the telephone in his typical no-nonsense tone. I only smile as I tip back my glass, the cool liquid making its way down my throat. I rise from the bar stool and glide out the door, feeling light as a feather.

Approximately thirty minutes later, I arrive at a building that looks as though it's been abandoned. Located in the seventh ward, the street the building inhabits seems to be scarce of any life. No pedestrians, no beggars, not even a sewer rat in sight.

I notice Kyle immediately. He seems to appear out of thin air, the fabric of his long, black trench coat seeming to drown him completely. He reminds me of a detective, ready to prosecute his perpetrator. I could fantasize about him all day. But not today. Today would be the day that I finally put his brother's case to rest. I could almost taste the sweetness of triumph. Kyle would soon have his revenge, and I, Kyle.

"This is it?" Kyle shoots me a puzzled look as we reach each other.

"Apparently so."

The building stands three stories high. Two of the French windows are poorly boarded up and the wood seems to be rotting. The house looks so frail that it would tumble down if pushed against in the slightest. The doorknob is missing and it takes hardly a push to open it with my heel. Dust scatters all around us and I cough, covering my mouth from the foul stench.

The dust settles and a grand staircase stands decaying in the center of the room. It looks as though it had once witnessed elegant evenings with proper gentlemen and ladies with their corsets fastened far too tight for them to breathe, only now to be housing common thieves. I'm sure it had once been a palace, having lived multiple lives with many owners whose hopes and dreams had come and gone with their arrivals and departures.

The farther we went into the house, the further it seemed to deteriorate, the walls stripped of any color or sign of liveliness and cockroaches infested in the floorboards beneath us. We reached Craven's door at the far end of the hallway. Even his door, compared to the others, seemed to embody a certain roughness that indicated it was resilient.

"Lucky thirteen," I say, eyeing the crooked thirteen embedded in the center of the door.

"I thought the number thirteen meant just the opposite."

"It does. I will go in first. It will be less intimidating if I go in on my own—especially being a woman, I pose less of a threat," I lie. We were hardly intimidating, especially to this man, I'm sure. I just couldn't have Kyle present when I interrogated him. My own agenda needed tending.

"No way. I'm going in there with you. I need to see him. I have to know if he's the one who—"

"I know, and you will," I say, placing my hand against his shoulder and looking deep into his eyes.

"You promised I'd get my revenge."

For a moment, I'm afraid he will go against me and make himself known to Craven too soon.

"I've gotten us this far, haven't I? Just hold onto your patience."

"Fine" — he scowls — "but just remember, it's running thin."

With that, he disappears down the hall, leaving me once again in control. I knock twice and wait, that thirteen making my skin crawl. The door opens and a man, larger than the door itself, stands before me. He smells foul, like a concoction of blood and sweat. He wears a dark, long button-down, matching trousers that are unraveling at the seams, and boots which look far too worn-out to still be intact. I look up at him, feeling like a doll, cowering and bright-eyed below him. I loathed that feeling more than life itself. I swallow, forcing myself to meet his mismatched eyes. One brown, one blue, just as John had said they would be.

"Nice eyes," I say.

"Who are you?" he growls.

"I want to hire you."

XVIII

A SHORT while later, I'm seated in a black leather chair across from Craven. He sits on the windowsill, or what seems to be left of it, as there are only shards of glass left crumbling around the edges. I wonder if he had pushed someone straight through it. Considering where we were, I doubt anyone would have noticed. The apartment was bare, housing no furniture besides the seat I assumed and a rusty, tarnished desk that stood between us. The space certainly left nothing to distract me from his frightening gaze.

"How old are you?"

I was taken aback for a moment before returning to reality where I was merely a fifteen-year-old girl. Of course, I wasn't, but in a way that was all I was.

"Does it matter?" I reply. A sly smile played on his lips.

"I don't do business with children."

"Good, because I'm hardly a child. Appearances are deceiving, would you disagree?"

"Not at all. I've noticed as much since I've arrived. I'm fairly new to the city."

"Yes. I've heard you have quite a ... reputation. For murder, that is." I said it as though it was a compliment. In New Orleans committing murder might as well be. He chuckled in his deep voice.

"Well, anyone can be a murderer. It only takes one time to go too far, slip over the edge."

Chills run down my spine and it's as if the lights seemed to dim, the room closing in on us. Noticing my uncomfortable reaction seems to please him.

"As ... as I was saying" — I clear my throat — "I'm looking to have someone taken care of."

He ignores me, continuing to taunt me with his questions.

"Have you ever owned a gun?" His eyes narrow at me.

"Of course I have," I reply, irritated. "This is New Orleans."

"How about a knife then?" I thought of the switchblade Kyle slipped in my pocket before I'd posed as a whore.

"What are you getting at?" I snap.

"Who would you like me to kill?"

He leans back a bit, the tension between us lingering.

"I—I..." I stammer as I press my palms into the leather of my seat, my mind spinning. It was rare when I was caught off guard. I cursed myself for not formulating a name and motive earlier. I'd relied too heavily on my ability to orchestrate lies easily. Time was ticking and I was becoming too hesitant.

"Have you ever held a butcher knife?" My body froze instantly, holding me hostage as my mind replayed the gruesome images of Luther laying cold and lifeless on his bathroom floor. I was taken aback, filled with fear, confusion, and blood—there was so much blood. Too much.

Craven dipped his head back, cackling at me. He was taunting me. He knew. He must have known.

"You're sick!" I spit out at him as I leaped up from the chair, placing both my hands on his desk, my eyes towering over him. He rises up from the windowsill, taking back the power with his broad shoulders.

"In truth, I should be thanking you for doing my job. But then again, you left a big mess. I would have just shot the poor son of a bitch in the head and called it a day. But to each their own, I suppose."

"That's why Luther was sent to Vex that night. He was sent to meet you."

Luther was meant to die before he'd even met me. His fate has been sealed long before I'd come along to only worsen the circumstances.

"Yes, but instead he met you. If I hadn't arrived twenty minutes later, his blood would be on my hands, as it was always meant to be."

Twenty minutes? That's what separated a life-changing occurrence in my life. It was overwhelmingly twisted. My stomach was turning over with regret, damning me for my drunken ways. A rush of anger washed over me as I watched him looking so smug. Like a child who had just gotten everything their way.

I jump onto the table, ripping the side of my chiffon dress, snarling at him. I shove him with all my force, but he barely budges an inch. The events that followed occurred so quickly that my mind couldn't comprehend. Kyle busted through the door, a mix of confusion and anger on his face. I realized how it must have looked. With me on the table, the tear in my dress, the viciousness of my body language. Craven, obviously startled, didn't have enough time to react from the blow of Kyle's fist meeting his face. He stumbled back, mouth gaping open as though he had something to say but there wasn't enough time.

Within seconds, Kyle pulled out a gun and shot him straight through the head. The sound of the shot made me lose my balance and I fell, crashing onto the floor below. I lay on the floor, my legs tangled and my fingernails digging into the wooden floor. I couldn't look up. I didn't want to see his brains scattered all over the room. I could smell the blood. The stench of blood is very specific. I couldn't explain it to you. It would be like trying to explain a color you've never seen before.

I felt Kyle's arms drag me off the floor. I buried my face in his chest, clinging onto him, waiting for it all to go away. I couldn't stand to see any more death, any more blood. I feared it would take over me completely. I kept my face buried in him as he shuffled down the stairs and scuttered out of the building. I didn't let my eyes open until we had left the street entirely.

XIX

KYLE places a cigarette between my lips. The scent of matches fills my lungs as he strikes one to light me up. We're lying side by side in his bed, white sheets tangled in between our bodies. He took me here after he had put a bullet in Craven's head.

I had done it. I had made it out alive once more. I had gotten away with murder. I should have felt like I was on top of the world, but I only felt lost. Kyle hadn't gotten the revenge he thought he had. The justice that Luther deserved had not come. It never would.

"What's the matter?"

Kyle strokes my golden locks, entwining his fingers between my curls. Droplets of water fall onto the sheets, as he had just finished bathing Craven's blood off his skin. He was so cool and content. I'd never seen him this way before.

"Nothing." I shake my head. "Are you sufficed?"

He seems pensive for a moment, perhaps wondering if it had felt as good as he had anticipated it would.

"No," he says surely. "My brother's still dead. But at least now I know his killer is in the ground alongside him."

I keep my face expressionless, fearing any sign might indicate he had killed the wrong man. I wonder if Craven's murder would haunt him the way Luther's haunted me.

"Have you ever killed anyone before?" I ask quite casually but with a sincere curiosity.

"No" — his head drops for a moment — "but I am not a murderer." I wouldn't have judged him if he had been. I was in no place to judge in that regard.

His eyes wander the room as I watch his mind working, justifying what he had just done which could not be undone. He was corrupt now, as I was. I suppose I should be pleased that he was now as horrid as I am, but I'm not. It is one thing to go through life being crude and spiteful and quite another to be a murderer.

I won't say I'm surprised—we are all capable of it, even the most innocent of us—but I wouldn't wish the burden of remorse for taking another life on anyone. And out of everyone, I wanted Kyle to be the last person in the city with some decency for human life, some morality left to show. I took his face in my hands and pressed my lips to his gently.

"No, you are surely not."

XX

I AWOKE early the next morning. The sun had snuck her way in through the curtains as though she was pleading for us to awaken. I loathed the daylight. Everything was too visible, too simply spotted. In the darkness, one could hide.

Kyle lies beside me, snoring softly, presumably still imprisoned in his dreams. I watch him for a while tossing and turning, his expressions shifting back and forth. I rise slowly and begin scouring the room in search of my ultimate vice, booze. Though, thinking of it now, it seems that Kyle may have become an even larger vice. It was strange how I could both detest him while simultaneously being willing to do anything in my power to keep him. I suppose that was the formula for creating a vice to begin with.

I chuckle at my foolishness while I raid the cabinets in his kitchen one after another until I find a bottle of gin hardly visible at the far back of the shelf. I snatch it stealthily, proceeding to take swings of it as I stumble around, hoping that Kyle's cramped, bare apartment may hold some answers to him.

One's room can often explain or even portray a person's life in various color schemes or trinkets left around for our amusement. Though, looking around, it seemed in his case it was quite the contrary. There was hardly anything to analyze.

In a strange way, his room reminded me of my own. There was nothing around to show myself to others, leaving it a mystery to figure out who I was or how I had come to be. We were the same, Kyle and I, made from the same mixture. Even our faults mirrored one another.

I heard music arise in my ears. It was a gentle and enticing melody, one I felt I had heard many times before. I close my eyes and feel hands grasping my waist, pulling me toward the center of the room. I look up to see Kyle, his hair ruffled, watching me dubiously. His eyes seem to carry a liveliness that they had not before. It was as though he had gone to sleep the night before and woken up altered in some way. A grin spreads across his face, causing me to smile in return.

"You are a secret romantic," I accuse him. He pulls me closer to him.

"Not anymore or any less than you."

Part of me wants to tell him I don't believe in love, but I don't want to ruin the moment. Kyle and I spend most of our time arguing and it feels comforting to just be. It was strange that everything was over.

"What are we to do now?" I ask.

"Whatever we want," he replies.

"But don't we do that anyways?"

"Yes."

I rest my head back onto his chest and let myself doze off into the music. I wish we could always be this way, but always is a very long time.

XXI

WHEN I eventually left Kyle's, I found myself grinning like an imbecile walking down the streets. The same dirty, piss- and blood-ridden streets that I had once stomped through and spit on, I now gracefully glided through. My logical mind scolded me for being so foolish, for replicating the traits of those that I had often despised in the past. I was a fool in love, but part of me did not care to be upset over it. I could not recall a time when I had felt so content and I knew how precious it was. How easily it could be taken away and replaced with a dim and soulless existence.

I had lived so long yearning for something real, something outside of a dimly-lit speakeasy or a night spent drowning myself with booze, and never thought I would actually find it. I reminded myself that this was merely a case of young love, all rushed and feverish and over all too quickly.

At last, I retired home and flung myself onto my bed. I was sick of getting wound up in my thoughts. Must I constantly ridicule and suspect the worst? Why couldn't I just be content? That's when I saw it. A scrap of paper had been set on my nightstand. I snatched it and read the carefully written handwriting:

"I KNOW WHAT YOU'VE DONE. I KNOW WHAT YOU ARE. MURDERER."

Chills ran up my spine as I bit down on my tongue reading the word "murderer." I swallowed the blood in my mouth as the word burned into my mind. My eyes wandered around my room as if wondering or waiting for someone to leap out and attack me.

What if this was from Kyle? Had he found me out? Maybe this was his way of taunting me, making me fall deeper in love with him only to kill me once he felt he had me well within his grasp.

No, Kyle was too forward, too brutally honest. If he knew, his impulses would have overtaken him the moment the information settled in his brain. He would have inflicted his revenge on me then and there if he knew.

The fear of the unknown was unbearable. Someone out there knew my darkest secret and was valiant enough to enter my home uninvited just to dangle it in front of me. The act of leaving the note had been a message in itself, giving away the fearlessness of its writer.

I was unsafe in my own home. My very bedroom had been corrupted.

There was nowhere to hide. Someone was coming for me.

XXII

I COULDN'T seem to get an ounce of sleep that night. I drained my last bottle of gin trying to drown out the paranoid voice that whispered endlessly of how my demise was near. When I could not stand it any longer, I relinquished the notion of sleep altogether and spent the rest of the night out on my balcony. I watched the sun rise, replacing the moon at dawn, my nightgown drenched in sweat from the humidity in the air.

I endured it as I smoked tirelessly, watching the ashes drift down into the streets below. I had almost forgotten how much I relished observing humanity from above, silent as a phantom, not a soul noticing me. As morning arrived, I wander downstairs and am startled by my father, whose frame appeared to fill the entire room.

He sat in the dining room reading the paper.

"Good morning, Alice," he says, not bothering to give me even a glance.

"Father," I reply, the hostility in my voice seeming to radiate through the walls.

"Sleep well?"

"Never," I respond.

"Well, try and rest today. Your presence is expected this evening." He spoke so matter-of-factly about everything. Always a demand, never an invitation. As though his words were the law. In this city, I suppose they are.

"What for?" I ask. He sets his paper down and raises his eyebrows at me.

"Tonight marks the New Year."

Had it come already? One of my father's largest nights of the year was tonight. Vex would be stocked with an enormous shipment of alcohol, barrels of booze stored in the cellar, and even more waiting in his warehouses lest they run out. The most coveted musicians would take the stage, flappers with the best moves would roam the floors below, and politicians and businessmen alike would be in attendance, all dressed in their finest and all eagerly anticipating the release of their inner desires.

"I suppose, I'll make an appearance."

"Good." He seemed pleased with my response. "I must go. I have much to do before tonight."

He left me with that.

XXIII

It was 1928, the start of a new year which I'm sure was to shatter more hopes and dreams of those who dare to dream at all. As it had been all the previous years, Vex was lively as ever. It had been ferociously cleaned, the countertops gleaming and not even a drop of liquor left on the floors. I arrived with approximately an hour until the clock struck midnight, having to shove my way through the crowds that lined up outside the doors. Walter gave me no trouble tonight, as he knew my father was expecting me. The band roared, the crowd was in a frenzy of dancing, and every glass was filled to the brim.

As I'm surveying the commotion, I knock into a curly-haired beauty with wild eyes. She shoots me an evil glare as I had just caused her to spill whiskey on her dress.

"Watch it," she snarls at me.

There were several men working the bar tonight to accommodate the large crowd, and with Jack nowhere in sight, I was left to find someone else to provide my fix. I approached a man nearest to me, who was sweating profusely, clearly overwhelmed.

"Bourbon, please."

He looked skeptical for a moment as he laid eyes on me, most likely wondering why there was a child in front of him demanding booze. Although judging from the looks of it, he didn't seem to be but a few years older than I.

"Is there a problem here?" I ask after a moment of not receiving a response, raising only an eyebrow to indicate any annoyance.

He merely smirked at me as he turned his back and went on grabbing various bottles and pouring their contents into glasses. I gritted my teeth impatiently, damning him as I stomped away, not willing to argue with an unfamiliar man. I darted past a few drunk flappers sprawled out on the floor as I turned the corridor, reaching the cellar. The cellar went deep beneath the club, the atmosphere of the world above disintegrating as I stepped down each decrepit step. Crates were stacked all around me, filled with various types of booze, causing me to salivate at the thought of it. I began to slide out a bottle when I noticed something between the crates. A body—a familiar body—lay on the floor only a few feet away from me.

"John?!" I exclaim.

I walked closer to find John's lifeless eyes staring up at me from the floor. His head was propped up against one of the crates while his body was bruised and his legs twisted in a sickening position. He was dead alright. I wondered if Jack had had him killed. I had only told them to beat him unconscious. Maybe they had killed him accidentally, beat him too bad that they didn't notice when he stopped breathing.

My speculation ended when I saw it. A bullet wound in his chest. I reached out, my fingertips tracing the wound. It was a perfect shot to the heart. I thought of the only man I know whose aim was that impeccable, Victor. I closed his eyelids and went back upstairs to find my father.

The spiral staircase leading to his office was blocked by one of his men. My father's men all looked the same and wore the same cold, hard expression. They moved to the side to let me through. I opened the door to the office to see my father dressed in his black suit with a white tie and a handkerchief in his pocket. He puffed on a cigar with one hand while the other had a glass half full of what I assumed was whiskey. He watched over the commotion through the window, as a wolf would its pack, examining each individual to be sure that they were behaving to his liking.

For as long as I could remember, my father spent most of the nights in his office, observing, away from the crowds. He would come down to greet a business partner or briefly greet the beautiful flappers who fawned over him, but then, just as soon as he had come, he would retire back to his office alone. I often wondered why he had opened a speakeasy to begin with if he took no interest in participating whatsoever.

"You've made it, I see."

"Yes," I reply smoothly. "I have."

"I informed Walter your presence would be required tonight."

"I assumed as much."

"I'm pleased to see you've managed to keep yourself composed tonight." He was referring to my drinking, of course. I didn't bother to mention it was due to the bartenders he hired and not my adamance to hold back. If I had known it would have been such an inconvenience, I would have arrived drunk.

"I thought you should know there's a corpse in your cellar," I say flatly. He makes a small frown.

"You aren't allowed in the cellar."

"And you aren't allowed to kill people, but here we are."

"You called upon my men for a job. I was simply finishing what you did not—protecting you, my blood, as I always have and always will do." I know I should have been grateful to my father for cleaning up yet again another one of my mishaps, but I was not. I can't stand to think of more blood being shed on my hands. I was not like my father, who had lost any regard for human decency a long time ago. In fact, I could never recall a time in my short life when he had.

"I did not kill him. I hire people for that, Alice." He said it as though it was the most moral thing in the world.

"You gave the word. Is that not the same to you?"

"It does not matter. That man was nothing but a nuisance." He did not care. He was not concerned with anyone but himself and his agenda.

"Is everyone disposable to you?"

"You are not saintly yourself. As I recall, it was you who made the demand to have him beaten into oblivion."

"I'm not a murderer." It escaped my mouth as merely a whisper.

"Oh, darling, but you already are." He exhaled, covering his face in a cloud of smoke.

I heard howling erupt from the party beneath us. The clock had struck midnight, the new year had come, and nothing had changed. Without another word, my father fixed his tie and left me alone with only my thoughts to keep me company. As he left, I realized I never got my drink.

XXIV

Smog blurs my vision as I find myself striding down the deserted streets several hours later on my way to Kyle's. After midnight struck, I'd spent the rest of the evening sulking alone, perched at my seat at the end of the bar. I'd watched the routine commotion of all the usuals at Vex get drunk until their legs wobbled and any indication of life had been drained from their faces.

I fantasized about Kyle mostly, and what was to become of us now that he was void of revenge. With him was the only time I felt spared from the harsh wards of time. Time did not exist with him. The past and future disintegrated into only a mere feeling of the present.

The crumbling, antebellum residences looked even more antiquated as the morning light began to shine on each one. The streets became filthier and the city was no longer booming with the energy from the night before, everyone presumably in bed recuperating from last night's festivities. As I approached Kyle's, I stop dead in my tracks, noticing a figure leave his building. He has a smirk on his face, as though he had just gotten away with the most sinister thing.

Damn him. It was Victor. His eyes meet mine as he takes the last step down before reaching the streets. I don't dare tear my gaze away from his. Our eyes remain locked until we are merely a few feet from one another. Victor looks clean and reserved as ever—not a single hair out of place. His button-down white shirt is crisp and pressed, his black slacks tucked neatly in and his shoes gleaming.

"Funny seeing you here," he says.

"A real joke," I reply belligerently. He takes another step toward me, if only to intimidate me with his height, towering over me.

"Care for a smoke?" he asks me. Tentatively, I nod, watching him reach into his pocket, producing Lucky Strikes and a matchbox. I lean in cautiously, allowing him to light me up.

"You shouldn't be roaming the streets at this hour. Could be quite dangerous." His words express concern, but his tone proves that he is only mocking me.

"You're assuming that due to my appearance?"

"Well, young girls should not be out on their own. It could lead to all sorts of unwanted ... occurrences, should we say?" A sly grin forms across his face as he exhales, emphasizing the word "occurrences."

"Why are you here?"

"Just paying a visit to a friend."

"You have a friend who resides in this building?"

"I do now, yes."

"What exactly are you getting at?" I ask, agitated and struggling to keep my composure.

"You know exactly what I am referring to. You are even more foolish than you appear if you think you could hide what you've done."

"You were the one. You wrote the note." I should have guessed. It was no wonder he had been daring enough to invade the privacy of my bedroom. Of all my father's men, Victor had been the only one allowed in our home.

"You seem dumbfounded, Alice. Does it bother you when you don't get your way?"

"You have no idea what you've done."

I felt as though the oxygen in the air was being constricted, causing my lungs to heave for air. He'd done it. He'd told Kyle the truth. I wanted to scream and cry and unleash myself onto him. I had done everything in my power to keep Kyle in the dark and Victor had so easily undermined me. The defeat I felt in that moment could compare to no other.

"Why did you do it?" I say, the anger coursing through my blood. "You are my father's most trusted ally, his right hand. Why do this?"

He laughed once more. "Your father is a no-good, rotten man who only cares for himself. He would sell me out in a moment if it was to his benefit." This was probably true. "You don't even know half of what he's done. The number of lives he has taken, the countless funds lost paying off every person in town. He's gone mad trying to attain some romantic fantasy!"

Romantic fantasy? What the hell was he referring to? My father was the coldest person I know. He couldn't possibly have a shred of romance.

"He was never the same after your mother died. He went insane, took it so far as to think he could bring her back. And now it's gone too far. He needs to be stopped."

Suddenly I recalled the love letter I'd found he'd written to my mother, how passionate and endearing it had been.

"Bring her back how?" I exclaimed.

Victor's voice lowered and his eyes darkened. "Clyde, Alice. With Clyde's help. When your father met him years ago, they shared a mutual interest. Clyde, being the demented physician he is, wanted to achieve the impossible, revival from the grave, and your father wanted his dear wife returned to him." It was all too twisted to comprehend.

"Then why ruin me? Why not just ruin him?" The moment the words escaped my mouth I knew the answer.

"You are his daughter, and your demise will be his greatest downfall. That's why."

Silence hung in the air between us. There was nothing more to say, nothing I could do now but live with the consequences of what I'd done. But maybe it was what I deserved. Yes, it was definitely what I deserved.

XXV

KYLE had found me out. I was a murderer. That was all—nothing more, nothing less. I held my knees against my chest, rocking back and forth, hidden in my closet, wishing more than anything that I could be anyone else in the world than who I was—that I had a loving father who wasn't a lunatic or that I myself was a person of decency. A person deserving of Kyle and his love, and a person who has all the things I ridicule in others. But instead, I am this—this vile, selfish thing. I truly was my father's daughter.

I couldn't even begin to think of the news of my father's involvement as well. In an attempt to avoid dwelling on the unfortunate events that had unfolded, I began the mundane routine of brushing out my honey blonde locks, powdering my cheeks, and plumping my lips, all while trying to hide my lifeless, sallow eyes.

My house was scarce of any life as I disappeared into the witching hour, leaving only the sounds of my Mary Janes clicking behind me. The city went on unaffected, the humidity in the air, the stench of the sewers, the beggars on the sidewalk. The only thing that had changed was me. My hope for happiness, any sort of happiness, was void. Any color the world once possessed had perished.

I turned corner after corner until reaching Vex. Walter stood at the door as usual and I darted through the clouds of smoke coming from flappers outside leaning against the walls, dolled up with pearls and extravagantly revealing outfits. Perhaps he noticed my morbid attitude because he let me in with no complaints. As I stepped through the door, I saw Jack wiping down the bar. His presence alone was comforting. At least that was something I knew would always be.

"Why, why, little Alice. What is the matter now?"

"Kyle despises me," I say, defeated, letting my face fall and be devoured by my hands. I wished I could hide from the world.

"Whatever for?"

"I wronged him." Jack looked at me compassionately as he fixes me a drink.

"You can be forgiven for your mistakes."

"Not this one. This one is unforgivable."

"Even the most appalling of crimes are forgivable."

"That has been true in the past, but I think I've lost everything this time," I say, downing the glass of gin.

"You've lost many things before."

"Nothing worthy enough to weep over until now, it seems."

"Perhaps it's for the best then."

"How could it be?"

"If he truly loves you, he will not be able to ignore it. His love for you will overpower any contempt he harbors."

"I'm not even sure if I believe in love. It seems like a ruse to me," I scoff.

"Don't the best things always seem that way?" he replies with a Cheshire cat grin.

I shrug, glancing up toward my father's office, his silhouette cast on the window as he paces back and forth, the smoke from his cigar trailing after him. I could not disregard what Victor had informed me of, as much as I willed myself to. It would be easy to tell myself that he was merely spewing lies, if only to avoid any more trouble within my life. But I craved the truth, the whole truth, and I figured now was as good of a time as any to confront him. I rose from the bar stool abruptly, stomping up the spiral staircase, determination rooted within each step.

"You said so hours ago! I was told it would be here at half past nine. Where the hell is it?" My father's voice reverberates throughout the room as I enter.

"I'm much too busy to listen to your excuses, now hurry the hell up!" He slams the telephone down violently. "Goddamn these men. They have one job, to transport the liquor, and they can't even manage that," he scoffs.

He exhales as he makes himself comfortable in his leather chair, which looks miniscule once he occupies it. His gaze rises finally, noticing me standing in the doorway. "Ah, Alice." His eyes light up slightly.

"Father," I say coldly.

"How is your night? Enough booze I presume?" His sarcasm irritates me, to say the least.

"Not nearly enough to deal with you." His eyes narrow.

"Is there a reason you're up here vexing me?"

I take a step forward, keeping my head held high. "I have a question actually," I reply.

"Regarding?"

"My mother." His hard expression falls a bit, but only for a moment.

"What about Elizabeth?" The way he says her name almost gave him away entirely. The shakiness in his voice, the vulnerability of even speaking her name.

"Why did you do it?"

"Do what?!" His tone harshened again.

"Why have you been conspiring with Clyde?"

"I don't know who you're referring to." He dismisses me as if I was an insect, beneath him and unworthy of his attention.

"Stop lying! I know about the body parts you've been importing from overseas and all the rest, so don't try and deny it any longer."

"You know nothing!"

The thundering of his screams fills my ears, paralyzing me with terror, waiting for the glass windows to shatter all around us or for the floor beneath us to crumble. He dashes across the room, taking hold of me, violently shaking me with tears welling up in his eyes. He was truly mad.

"Why can't you let her be? She can't come back." I whisper.

"She can, and she will," he says firmly. "There is no other way to live on, if

I thought she could not." His grip loosens and his breath slows, providing me with the opportunity to tear myself out of his grasp, increasing the space between us.

"She took her own life, father. There was nothing you could do."

"There was everything I could do, but I did not. Fortunately, there is no need to dwell on past blunders, seeing as she will be returning to us soon. One day, you will understand, Alice, that when you love someone, there is no life without them."

I thought of Kyle, causing my heart to ache.

"I think I do understand, father." My life had changed the moment I met him. I don't think I was ever truly alive until the day I met him.

"I know the boy you're speaking of, and he will never forgive you for what you've done." His words were equivalent to that of a stab wound, painful and left open for the world to see. I should not be surprised that he had known of Kyle all along. My father has eyes everywhere.

"I know," I respond solemnly. "And I'm not sure how I'll ever recover."

"We have to get rid of him, Alice, before he comes for you." I anticipated he would come to this conclusion, but anticipating and being confronted with the notion were two vastly different concepts.

"You can't!" I exclaim. "You can't! I need him. He's the one, the only one."

"I'm done dealing with your indiscretions."

"I know father," I reply apologetically.

"Which is why I'm not going to kill him, Alice. You are."

XXVI

I KNOW there are moments in each of our lives when we must do things we don't want to. I can say I've had my fair share of unwillingness to comply with what was demanded of me, but never quite like this. I'm not sure exactly how many people have been in the position where they have to kill someone that they are in love with, but I'm assuming most haven't. It's not because they are incapable, by any means—I'm sure they are—but the idea is so excruciating, I think any rational person would choose whatever else they had to deal with instead. Even if it meant dying themselves.

But my father was right. Kyle could never love me—not now, anyway. I can imagine him now, in his apartment pacing back and forth, filled with the utmost anger and hatred for me boiling inside him. I reach for my bottle of gin and gulp down as much as I can take. I'm lying at the foot of my bed, bottle in hand, shaking with fear, paranoia, and shock. He's coming for me. I drink more. I drink until the bottle runs out and the next bottle and until I can feel my head pounding so hard. It was past midnight now. The witching hour had arrived and it was time to end this once and for all.

The house is dark and empty as it usually is, the furniture untouched as always, and I go to my father's closet. His bedroom is organized, everything exactly as it should be. The very opposite of mine. He has trays filled with cigars and his sheets are always freshly cleaned and made up. I can't remember the last time I even washed mine.

My eyes scan down through his drawers to the one at the very bottom where I know he keeps his pistols. I grab the lightest one and just sit there, holding it in my hand for just a moment, wondering just how far I'm willing to go to save myself. Why would I even save myself? I should just let death come for me. But somewhere, deep inside me, I know I wouldn't let myself do that. Human instinct is to survive at all costs: predator and prey. I had to be the predator. I had to prevail.

I rummage through my father's clothes, throwing on one of his dinner coats which looks gigantic on my petite frame, and pair it with a set of black leather gloves and a top hat. I didn't even bother glancing at my appearance before scurrying down the stairs and out into the cold night. I was grateful to be so heavily intoxicated that I could only focus on getting there. If I tried to put my mind to much else, I would surely get lost or end up in a frenzy.

Kyle's was close, but at that moment I wished it could be an eternity away. His building came into view. The street was silent; the air was cool on my skin. I peered around me, making sure not a soul in sight would see me. I walked carefully up the steps, shoving the main door to his building open and reaching his door. I quickly picked the lock and opened it as gently as I could.

It was pitch-black with only the moon shining through his thin curtains down onto his sleeping body. He looked so peaceful as he slept, his hair ruffled and in only his trousers. I held the gun in my hand, stagnant at the door, just watching, the tears slowly welling up in my eyes. Why did death seem to follow me everywhere? Why was I constantly surrounded by it, myself and others taking crucial roles in ending other people's existence? Living, breathing human beings who could have had an endless possibility of outcomes to their lives. And Kyle, the only one who understands me, my lover, my companion—just look at what I was doing to him now.

I began shaking as I hear my father's voice screaming in my head. "He doesn't love you. He cannot love you. No one ever could." I whisper it to myself as I raise the gun and aim it at his chest. My vision is blurry and it takes every ounce of my being to pull the trigger. The shot rings so loud I stagger to the desk nearby. I see blood seeping deep into the sheets. I hear shuffling coming from the apartment next door, voices of neighbors. People are coming.

I want to stay with him, run to him, hold him in my arms, but I cannot. I force myself to leave, tearing my eyes away from his bloody body and dashing down the stairs as fast as my feet will carry me. I stumble from wall to wall, out the door, and continue stumbling into the street. I feel so ill my stomach gives out and I proceed to vomit all over myself. I stare up at the moon in the sky, hopeless.

"How could this happen? How could I become this way?"

I continue to vomit, making the most atrocious sounds. The moon just looks down at me, gleaming, still and unaware of my obvious cry for help. I suppose in moments such as these, there is no next step to take, no place to go home to and cry. I had no one to go to. Not even the moon, my precious moon, wanted me anymore.

XXVII

"Ah, death, the cure of a lifetime! I'm sure the local asylum would surely admit you if you asked nicely enough."

"I'm not a nice girl," I reply.

"More of a reason they would admit you, I suppose," Baxter replies.

He smokes an antiquated brown pipe. It looked so old, most of the wood had been chipped from it. I could barely comprehend how it was still intact. He is an old fellow, I would assume in his early sixties, a beggar who regularly resides in Jackson Square, accosting passersby for money. His hair is gray, what remains of it anyway, and his lungs presumably black from years of smoking. In short, he was me in fifty or so odd years. If I manage to make it that far, that is.

It's been a few days since I'd murdered Kyle. I met Baxter the morning after I'd killed him. I've spent the past few days here with him, in my father's coat, which still has my dried vomit all over it, unbathed, and completely lost of any sanity.

"Miss," he croaks out to a woman passing by. "Would you be so kind to help me out with a few cents?" The woman looks of the upper class, wearing a long green coat with what seems to be real fur trimming. She looks repulsed at the sight of him.

"Don't come near me, vagrant."

He merely looks over at me and shrugs, continuing to puff on his pipe. Clouds of smoke formulate around us as we sit side by side on the cobblestone pavement, which reeks of decades of filth due to the residents of the city.

"As I was saying, Alice, a friend of mine was a real mess and he was able to get admitted and now he seems much better."

"Yes, I've been seriously considering it recently. What exactly would it entail?"

"Well, there would be a fine doctor, who would wear a white lab coat and have expensive spectacles. He would have good manners and be very sympathetic to the unfortunate circumstances which brought you to him."

"I never trusted doctors," I say. "They always seem too ... something."

"Well, this one would be different. You would take a liking to him immediately. He wouldn't be like any other doctor you've met before." His eyes gleam with an otherworldly gaze.

"Alright, I may give him a chance," I say reluctantly.

"He would listen to your story, taking notes on his clipboard, nodding and analyzing in his mind if you are a good candidate to be admitted. Then, once he decided you were, he would bring you into an all-white room with no windows. The room would be inhabited by nothing except for a metal bed frame with a thin mattress and restraints for your wrists and ankles. Naturally, they do this to prevent you from hurting yourself or another patient if you are to have a fit."

"Naturally," I say.

"Next, a beautiful nurse would enter the room. She would be tall, slim, and have the most vivacious smile. She'd be wearing a long, white linen dress, stockings, and a nursing cap. She would be so enchanting that you would want to stay forever in this asylum just to be able to catch glimpses of her every day. She would be darling, but professional, and would tend to your every need. Your days would consist of medical and psychological analyses, doctors, nurses, and interacting with other patients. There would be difficult days of course, where another patient may try to harm you or you to another patient."

"I would probably be the patient doing the harm," I say flatly. Baxter laughs.

"Yes, and the beautiful nurse would then be forced to restrain you to your bed or possibly put you in a straitjacket. But it would only be temporarily until you calmed down, and then you would be released and no one would hold your tantrum against you."

"That sounds awfully nice. Perhaps too nice to be real." A place where you could just let the insanity run free, no one to punish you for your wrongdoings. It reminded me of my father, how every single fault and mistake I made was constantly relayed to me. The constant ridicule of my behavior, which in truth was valid, was still undeniably hurtful.

"It is certainly real. As I said, a friend of mine went and he is now in much better condition."

"How is he better now?"

"He's dead now, Alice."

My brows furrow, confused. "I don't understand. You said he recovered."

"He did. As I said to you in the beginning of the story, death is the cure of a lifetime."

A sly grin spreads across his face as he winks at me. I laugh, thinking that this beggar seems to be the most intelligent person I've encountered in a long time. It is certainly sad to see how the world could miss out on his potential, just because he hasn't bathed in a while or doesn't own a wallet. Who even cared about such—

"Audrey?!" I heard someone screech from behind me.

Startled, I turn around and, oddly enough, it was Rose, the little brunette from the brothel whose temper tantrums most likely qualified her to be in a mental asylum. Her hair was curled, face perfectly made up, and she had her hands so full of shopping bags she was practically tipping over. Her blue eyes looked astonished to see me in such a filthy state, and I'm sure sitting next to Baxter wasn't doing me any favors as well.

"Audrey, baby, come here," she waved from across the street, her expression beginning to look further and further worrisome. I pick myself up off the street, wandering over to her.

"Audrey, you reek! Are you alright?" It was clear she was trying to hide her disgust. I was obviously not alright.

"I suppose," I reply. She raised her eyebrows.

"Who's that man you're with? He looks unsanitary..." I shrug.

"Aren't we all, in some way or another?" She doesn't understand my joke. I didn't expect her to either.

"How long have you been out on the street?" she asks.

"Few days, I think."

"Honey, come on back to Clyde's with me. The automobile's just over here. I'll get you cleaned up in no time."

I look back at Baxter smoking his pipe alone, being ignored by everyone around him. I don't want to leave him. He was amusing and I think he enjoyed my company as well. But being in a rather unpleasant state, I figure he would have to fend for himself. After all, he'd made it this far. I gave him one last apologetic glance before letting Rose steal me off with her back to Clyde's.

XXVIII

By the next hour, it seemed I was in a completely new state—physically, I mean. Mentally, I was too far gone to be salvaged. I was soaking in the tub, all the vomit and dirt scrubbed off my skin, surrounded by Rose, Ivy, and Adrianna. We were in the luxurious bathroom of the bedroom I stayed in the last time I was here and it was as breathtaking as I remembered. Almost better now. The steam seemed to rise all around the room as Ivy sat on one of the love seats brushing out her elegant red curls. Adrianna sat adjacent to her smoking cigarette after cigarette, seeming more bored than anything.

"You definitely look much better," Ivy says, putting down the comb and moving on to powdering her cheeks.

"Certainly does. There was no chance in hell I was going to leave her there on the street with that old man!" Rose exclaims proudly as she begins to wash my hair.

"Old man?" Adrianna says, her attention seeming to be piqued.

"A beggar I met," I say casually. Ivy and Adrianna seem to express the same amount of distaste as Rose had. Rose seems to be used to it by now. The shock wore off, I suppose.

"You are much too lovely to be with a man like that. Don't sell yourself short," Adrianna says.

"It wasn't like that. He was just keeping me company," I respond.

"Well, don't tell Clyde that. He doesn't let men keep us company for free in his house," Ivy says curtly. I laugh, remembering I was in a whorehouse.

"Yeah, if we did, we'd never have any free time at all," Rose chimes in while giggling behind me.

I reach for a towel and begin drying myself off. I smell of lavender-scented soap and my skin was radiating. Ivy hands me a blood red slip and a fresh pair of stockings to wear as Ivy helps powder my cheeks and Rose sprays me with perfume. When I am finally done, I peer at myself in the body-sized mirror. It felt as though I was admiring a body that didn't belong to me. I look the same as I always had, my honey blonde hair, my sharp cheekbones, my pout, my hip bones which could never manage not to stick out, but inside something had changed.

I'd been managing to keep myself from thinking about Kyle for as long as I could since that night occurred. I knew I had to do it. It was me or him. If I hadn't come for him, it would have only been a matter of time before he came for me. I kept reminding myself over and over that the second he found out about the vile, atrocious thing I'd done, he would have lost any and all feeling he had for me. It was the only way I could cope with what I'd done.

"There," Adrianna says, interrupting my thoughts as she puts a long string of pearls around my neck. "All done. Now, let's go find a man who will fall madly in love with you." My expression stays blank, staring at myself. After all, how could anyone love a murderer?

XXIX

THE night dragged on as I expected it would. Men came and left, politicians, gamblers, businessmen, the usual mix. All evening, the men danced, smoked, and drank with the girls, laughter constantly echoing throughout the rooms. I sat on an emerald green love seat with a mahogany wood finish, my legs sprawled out in front of the fireplace, my eyes fixated on the sparks. I'd been in this exact spot all night, downing as much booze as I could and giving the cold shoulder to anyone who attempted to strike up a conversation with me.

I hear a boisterous laugh erupt from across the room and look over to see it had come from Clyde. His light brown hair was perfectly combed back, his black suit, waistcoat, and tie all nicely pressed. He looked lively, handsome, and so alluring. The kind of man any woman would swoon over in a heartbeat.

But I knew his secret, the web of lies hidden beneath his bewitching facade, his maniacal plans for bringing the dead back to life. Physicians always seem to be so high and mighty, thinking they're of some godly breed of humans. I wonder why he even bothered to pretend he cared about anyone in this room at all, or even this house for that matter. It must be exhausting for him to keep up niceties with everyone, while simultaneously hiding his true intentions. Truth be told, I couldn't care less about what he was plotting. The only thing I had cared for, the only person, was dead, at my hands no less. If that did not make me worse than him, I'm not sure what would. Clyde was just another madman in a city filled with other madmen, really not far-fetched from the rest of us.

It was as though he could hear my thoughts, because moments later he glanced over at me and smiled. I did not offer one in return, instead keeping on the grim expression I had occupied all night. He excused himself from the group of men who surrounded him and walked over to me.

"Not entertained tonight, are you?"

"No," I reply, peering down at my near-empty glass.

"Let's get you another drink, shall we?" His eyes glisten as he attempts to charm me. He reaches his hand out to me and I reluctantly allow him to pull me from my seat.

"Fine," I say with obvious annoyance in my voice. He leads me through the swarm of lit cigarettes, lively faces, and lavish decor into a room I had not discovered: the library. Books fill the walls all around us. It must have been thousands on thousands, organized neatly on their shelves. I run my hands over some of the books, noticing many of them have titles related to science, anatomy, or medicine—unsurprisingly so. Clyde pours me a glass of bourbon from a set of fine bottles on a nearby tray.

"You like to read?" he asks.

"Not really," I say. "My father never approved of it much. He also never read to me as a child or anything of that nature."

It slipped out, the mention of my father. Now that I knew of their connection, I was almost certain he must know of my true identity. He kept his cool demeanor though. After all, he had done so in the past when I was here.

“That’s a shame. There are such fine novels out there. You don’t know what you’re missing,” he mused.

“I suppose I should try it,” I consider. “I’ve missed out on so many things already.” It was a broad statement, one which I had meant in many forms.

“Such as?” he asks.

“I feel as though I’ve missed out on everything a child reminisces on when they grow up.”

“You’re still a child. There’s still time,” he says optimistically.

“No.” I look directly at him, my eyes lifeless. “I’m not anymore. Let’s not pretend, shall we?”

I’m much too exhausted to play games any longer. He shifts his body uncomfortably, breaking his gaze from mine.

“Audrey, I don’t want you to lose hope. That is all I am intending. The world is changing with each passing moment and oftentimes the most unexpected gifts can be the ones right in front of us.”

“You don’t have to call me that anymore,” I respond. “I know you know who I am.”

He sets down his drink, his charming demeanor shifting into something quite unrecognizable. Yes, Clyde, put down the facade and let me see you in your true flesh. I want you to reveal the devil underneath.

“Okay then, Alice. Is that how you would prefer to be addressed?”

"Call me whatever pleases you. A name is just a name, either way. I'm just sick of playing pretend with you. I know what you're up to with my father." His eyes seem to light up as he forms a wicked grin. He comes closer to me, lowering himself so he is able to whisper in my ear.

"You think you know it all, don't you?"

"I know enough." He laughs loudly again, as he had when we were in the living room, but this one seems to echo even further off the walls.

"You should be thanking me. With your father's assistance, I will be able to bring your mother back. Maybe she will be the one to finally talk some sense into you."

"Perhaps, seeing as nobody around here seems to have any," I reply, "especially you." The spite slipped off my tongue so easily.

"You want to know what I think? I think you don't want her to come back, because you know how ashamed she'd be of you. Her daughter, a known drunk and a lunatic."

I couldn't stop myself from spitting in his face. I can't believe I ever thought he was charming at all. His face looked up at me with such rage, causing me to turn as quickly as I could, attempting to run. He caught my wrist as I turned and I dropped my drink, the sound of shattering glass piercing the air. He howled and fell to the ground.

Part of me wanted to see where the glass had cut him, but the crash left me with only enough time to escape. I ran through the library back into the living room, past the bright faces and dimly lit candles, until I dashed out the door, knowing I would never return.

XXX

Home. The word seemed more meaningless now than it ever had before as I sat in the dining room of the home off Royal and Bourbon, where I've resided my entire life. The place where I've wept, wallowed, and contemplated the many horrors and delights I've encountered within the span of my fifteen years.

After I'd dashed home last night, I'd waited for Clyde to come for me. Each time I'd heard a creak or a movement of a shadow beyond the windows, I was sure he'd come barging through the door at any moment.

The look in his eyes, the unspeakable rage, the way he seemed to shapeshift into a completely different being within a moment had shaken me. I'd never witnessed an evil overcome a man so completely and I was sure he would not be able to resist the urge to come after me.

I guess I'd been wrong, because I'd waited and he had never come. Maybe part of me wanted him to come after me, end it all, so I would not have to live with myself any longer. It feels daunting now, having to deal with any aspect of life at all. I have neither the strength nor the willingness to carry on as I have.

I allow my head to rest on the table, my body craving the sleep I've denied myself for far too long. My breath slows and my eyelids proceed to close, welcoming the escape from the torture of my thoughts. A few moments later, a chime at the door startles me and I stumble to the window to see that the post has arrived. I mundanely go to retrieve it, only to notice my name inscribed neatly on one of the letters.

Suspicious and quite frankly distraught at the prospect of yet another dose of unpleasant news, I'm tempted to dispose of it without another glance. Then again, it could surely not surpass the terrors I'd endured. Ruthlessly, I rip it open, the shreds of the envelope scattering around my feet as I read it.

Dear Alice,

How can I begin to comprehend the awful acts you've committed? My world was demolished upon your arrival, and at the time, it seemed that no room was left for anything but hatred and rage. And it was that which filled me so, dwelling inside as a demon would, waiting hungrily with wide eyes and sharp fingernails for the opportunity to avenge my brother. I understand only now that it would never fill me, even for a brief moment when I believed it had. I would have never suspected it was you—not because I think you are incapable, but because even amongst all my pessimistic ideations, I held onto the notion that there was some good within the world. I genuinely wish Victor had not told me the truth so we could have gone on the way we were. The day he came to me, delivering the truth, was nearly as gut-wrenching as the day I found Luther's cold and lifeless body. I wish it could have been anyone but you. But as we always say, there is no room in this horrid city for anything good to last too long. I myself have been corrupted by it, as you have. The pain and suffering seem to be in the air, catching us one by one like a ravenous disease. It's infected us all and now all that is left to do is to forgive one another and leave our faults behind. I've come to the conclusion that this is the only cure. In some way, knowing the darkest parts of you draws me to you further, as a moth to a flame. I can't find it inside myself to hold onto this hate any longer. You are what I have been searching for, Alice, and if I lose you, I will be left with nothing but the nostalgia of the past taunting me. I'm not sure when you will receive this, but when you do, know I will be waiting by the Mississippi for you at midnight. I'll wait every night until you come.

Yours truly,
Kyle

XXXI

The full moon seemed to consume the entire city, lighting up even the darkest parts of the street as I dragged myself down block after block, passing all the most historic streets that I'd known for the entirety of my short life. Royal, Bourbon, Decatur—one after another, they remained undaunted by their surroundings. The streets here had witnessed their residents commit the most unfathomable crimes, murder being only one of the few. I wondered if they would notice my absence, perhaps wondering where that deranged young girl had disappeared off to. I doubted so. After all, who would care to notice the absence of a young girl who had filled the world with nothing but more destruction.

I'll pretend they will, though, for the mere sake of wanting to be missed, even if it's just by the streets themselves. I only wish that they will fondly hold the memory of Kyle and me together as we had been when we had stormed these streets, hand in hand, enemies and secret lovers.

I was stunned by his words, to say the least. How could he be so forgiving? I suppose that's what true love is, loving someone no matter what they've done, no matter how vile or horrific their actions may be, choosing to see the good in them even when they are blind to it.

I looked at myself and could see no goodness in me, but Kyle saw it, or perhaps the potential to be good. It only made the pain worse, and my love for him grew. I'd wronged him more than one could possibly ever wrong another. I'd killed his only brother and then killed him in an attempt to save myself from him, when in truth he was never coming for me.

The only person who I needed protection from was myself. I was my own captor, my own demon in the flesh, taunting myself. I only wish I would have allowed things to unfold as they were meant to. I have always assumed the worst of the world, fixating so certainly on the belief that everyone and everything is a threat. Trust no one, abide by no one, you are your only protection and your only salvation. I would like to blame my father, but it would solve nothing. It would bring neither Kyle nor Luther back.

I scurried down to the rocks, looking over the Mississippi, the water calm and swaying. I flung my shoes off and climbed down each crooked, sharp rock until I was standing above the edge of the water. I peered down at the murky river, imaging the monstrous alligators among other sorts of creatures that inhabited it. I surrender control of my body to the river, letting myself fall in.

It was effortless and rather relieving to surrender control—surrender control of my body and my mind to something other than myself. I closed my eyes as the river clutched me, holding me tightly in its grasp, dragging me deep down into its arms. I deserved this. I'd done Kyle so wrong, it only seemed fair that I was sentenced to the same fate.

I think my life was always supposed to end this way, drowned in the river. It was the only way I could ever escape the cruel wards of time or the corruption that surrounded me. The corruption I could not seem to shy away from, constantly going back for more—more pain, more destruction—chipping away at myself and anyone who dared walk in my path.

I thought of my father, who I always deemed to be so strong and invincible, but now I could see how desperate he was. All the years he spent building his empire, the booze, the money, the countless women. It was all an act. His love for my deceased mother fueled his delusions to the point where he actually believed he could bring her back. She was his hope for living, just as Kyle had been mine.

In a strange way, I was relieved to know that, no matter how absurd he may be, my father really did have a heart beating in his chest. For so long, I was certain that there was nothing under his rib cage or between his lungs. I wondered if, perhaps, everyone needed someone to live for. A lover to fantasize about, a companion to share their world with, no matter how shattered that world may be. A person to call home when even the most decadent of houses seem to be just large rooms filled with things.

It felt as though my sins were being washed as I sunk deeper toward the bed of the river. Maybe they were. After all, we must all pay for our sins sometime and I am most certainly a sinner. Some of us are not made to do good for the world; some of us were created to cause havoc, and I am certain now that I am among those. The devil always returns to those who were once his and now, at last, I am being returned to him.

Grace Hannah Perez was a true-blue artist in all respects. She used her voice across many forms of creative expression from writing to painting and the modeling of clothing. She was enamored with all things miniature, printing a number of her stories in the form of tiny books. Her aesthetics drew from both fashion and history, inspired by Marie Antoinette and Coco Chanel.

Perez loved creating magic through her stories. Highly imaginative, she was a voracious writer and reader. She kept a journal, assiduously transforming her life into writing. Yet she lived for the moment—a prolific trance dancer, music lover, faerie spirit, Perez charted her life beneath the movement of the stars. As a Taurus sun, Gemini rising, and Sagittarius moon, she was an alchemist of potions and herbs, often wreathed in the scents of lavender and rose. Her favorite weather was rain, her favorite colors green and purple. Perez enjoyed traveling the world, including to her favorite city, New Orleans—a city whose stories of the 1920s captivated her and which she refigures in this novel.

An old soul, Perez was born on the full moon of May 18, 2000 in Los Angeles, California. Honoring her Sephardic Jewish heritage, Perez bat-mitzvahed with her sister Ava Perez in Jerusalem. She was a hopeful romantic with a kind, open heart. Full of wit and the keen sense of humor evinced here and in all her projects, she was loving and loved as a daughter, a sister, and a loyal friend. On March 14, 2023 at twenty-two years of age, Grace Hannah Perez ascended into the heavens on a waning gibbous moon.

Made in the USA
Monee, IL
22 May 2024

63aac229-0b08-46e8-af4d-b7e95fe8d2ceR02